ROO AND THE NORTH BURROW

Roo and the North Burrow
Copyright © 2024 by Carrie A. Keller

Published in the United States of America

Library of Congress Control Number: 2024921708
ISBN   Paperback: 979-8-89091-728-7
ISBN   eBook: 979-8-89091-729-4

All rights reserved. No part of this publication may be reproduced, stored in a retrieval system or transmitted in any way by any means, electronic, mechanical, photocopy, recording or otherwise without the prior permission of the author except as provided by USA copyright law.

The opinions expressed by the author are not necessarily those of ReadersMagnet, LLC.

ReadersMagnet, LLC
10620 Treena Street, Suite 230 | San Diego, California, 92131 USA
1.619. 354. 2643 | www.readersmagnet.com

Book design copyright © 2024 by ReadersMagnet, LLC. All rights reserved.

Cover design by Tifanny C Curaza
Interior design by Don De Guzman

Roo and the North Burrow

CARRIE A. KELLER

Roo and the North Burrow

Crum (kram, krum) n.

Crum, an evolutionary off-shoot of Hominidae, a species of homo-sapiens. They have hidden and thrived in the great old forests since the days of cavemen. At full adulthood a Crum is no more than thirteen inches tall. They are tough, intelligent, and quite strong. Their grey-brown coloured skin and green hair allow them to blend seamlessly into the landscape. They can hear the thoughts of animals and communicate with them. Crum have the appearance of humans except for very large eyes for seeing in the burrow's dim light, small flattish noses, have ear holes instead of ears, and wide, smiling mouths. A Crum clan normally live in great burrows dug under giant trees that they call, *'Home Tree.'* The many rooms and halls of the burrow are made habitable with smooth stone and carved wood. The burrow is illuminated by phosphorescent mushrooms that have been cultivated in niches along its walls. The average population of a home tree burrow is seventy-plus Crum. With a diet of small proteins such as insects and every edible plant on the forest floor, they can live approx. two hundred years if allowed to die naturally. Crum hibernate over winters, and every spring they emerge from their burrow to forage, stretch their sleepy muscles, clean out the winter bedding, and clear away the winter seasons' detritus left around the *Home Tree*.

The ancient wood has just awakened from the winters grasp, trees are pulling up the sap and pushing out their hungry buds to catch the strengthening rays. Mammal and avian sing and frolic in the open branches, the music of life has been turned up to full volume. At the forest floor the activity is multiplied, though the activity is not as obvious to the eyes of creatures living in the heights. The insects are immerging, the seeds and roots that have been waiting patiently are pushing up through the mulch and the sloughed-off leaves of last year. And the Crum have pushed open the doors of the multi-roomed burrow that weaves around the roots of the great oak tree, airing and activity making the passages crowded and busy as a beehive.

CHAPTER ONE

THE SHUM HARVEST

The squirrel, glossy and black, shivered with anticipation and caution, edging closer to the pine nut that Mar held out to her. "Come on, you know you want it", she coaxed.

"My favourite!" Thought the squirrel and Mar heard his thoughts as clear as if he had spoken.

"I know!" said Mar.

Its dark eyes widened with the realization that this green haired and grey skinned creature could speak to him and hear him. Small black paws darted forward to grab the nut. She laughed in her delight, eye to eye with the rodent.

Mar's twin sister called back to her, "Hurry up and stop feeding the squirrels our lunch!" Par, like her, had dark green waves of hair above large golden eyes that they had inherited from their mother. It was the personalities that were different- Mar was cheerful and thoughtful, Par was fierce and wild. At twenty-nine they were still younglings, just old enough to not need supervision but not to be trusted outside of the Crum- watched territory. Bip and Ryn held hands where space allowed as they walked behind their prodigy, while also keeping in view the rabbit who was bringing the harvest baskets strapped to her sides. Partners for ages, they still felt that the yearly outing was a romantic break from the crowded bustle of Home Tree.

The squirrel leaped away, tail flipping. Mar ran up to Par as she strode confidently, waving a sharpened stick in front of her. "When we get back to Home Tree, I'll ask Roo to help me make a real stone-tipped spear!" She said, looking determined. Mar rolled her eyes at her sisters' combative nature." What do you want with that, you can't be a watcher yet and you can't hunt on your own!" Weaving through the forest undergrowth they pushed at leaves the same size as their rosy cheeked grey faces, the hazy spring vault of sky promising to stay warm and clear. They dodged the new spouts coming through the dense layers of last year's leaves, the familiar heavy smell of earth and fungi surrounded them as a cacophony of bird song played overhead.

The family were makers of the, "shums", a garment that all the Crum wore. The ever-useful cowl-cape was dyed in a camouflaging pattern to match the ancient temperate forest they lived in. They were on their yearly gathering expedition, one days walk southwest of the great oak, Home Tree, and the clan's burrow. The Burrow: Cleverly concealed and multi-levelled, with a beautiful front entrance door set between two huge roots. Inside, the many rooms amongst the roots were walled with carved and shaped wood and well-worn but clean stone floors. The Crum have perfected the living in harmony with the tree and all their forest environment, being able to communicate with animals intertwined their lives with all woodland creatures.

At midday they halted at a fresh-let stream, one of the many that fed into the Home Tree creek. Everyone drank the delicious cold water, even the rabbit gulped eagerly before moving away to graze at a grassy tuft. Balancing on a mossy rock, Bip removed his backpack and distributed the leaf bundles of pine-nuts and creamy grubs before taking out one large strawberry. Taking his stone knife from the mouse-leather satchel, he divided it into four chunks that each of the Crum needed two hands to hold.

All Crum had various shades of green hair and one expressive green brow, tough grey-toned skin, and large luminous eyes that could see well in the dim tunnels of the burrow. Along with the shums draped around their necks, Crum wore leather clothing made from small rodents. One difference between male and female dress is most females added a light-coloured suede tab apron over their torsos held close with a long slim leather belt.

Bip, unlike his mate and younglings, had dark green eyes under a heavy brow and new-leaf green curls. "We've had a great day to do this, I hope that we'll have time to cut some shum bark before dark." He said, as he swung his now lighter pack on again. "Mar and Par, you can start looking for the dye plants, there should be some outside the grove." The twins nodded, having been on this trip every spring that they could remember.

Both Ryn and Bip carried a good stone tipped spear in one hand, the carrying straps hanging loose, ready to be slipped across their backs when not needed. All adult Crum carried a spear and sometimes a watch-pipe when away from Home Tree. The pipe gave a piecing sound when blown that all animals found painful, the spear was good only for a sharp poke in an eye or nose when a stubborn animal needed further dissuading from biting. Crum skin secreted a foul-tasting enzyme, but a strange animal wouldn't know that until the damage of a bite had already happened. That was why the clan had "Watchers" duty: someone always manned the territories border trees to call warnings.

Suddenly the rabbit hopped close, calling, "Danger!" His simple thoughts heard clearly by the four Crum. The twins gathered close around Bip and Ryn, with the trembling rabbit trying unsuccessfully to disappear behind them, it's fur-ball body twice the size of the Crum. Rustling bushes parted, the face of a very young bobcat slipped out, hungrily looking at their rabbit. Ryn held a watch pipe to her mouth, ready to blow it while Bip challenged the cat: "Leave our friend, find your food elsewhere!" It stopped, tilted his grey furred face, comical tufts on his ears wiggling. "You must be Crum; I've heard of you from a fox that lets one of you ride on him." The cat sat down nonchalantly and began cleaning a paw pad with a raspy tongue. Par moved from behind Bip: "That must be Fen! Roo rides on him when they hunt!"

"I am called Tich."

"My name is Par, and this is my sister, Mar, my Deda is called Bip, our Mema is Ryn. We are on a shum gathering."

The bobcat was amused at the matching younglings. "I'm not really hungry anyway, just ate a fat rat." He licked at his chops and blinked at the twins. They could hear the happy purr as the bob cat smoothly flowed back into the brush, hardly shaking a leaf.

"Oh, yuck!" said Mar.

They noticed the bob cat keeping pace with them but not coming closer. The shadows were lengthening when the Crum came into the grove of smooth barked shum trees. Bip released the baskets from the rabbit but asked him to stay close; their nervous helper quickly squashed himself into a small, hollowed log, face out. They would be staying the night in the grove and walk back in the morning. Ryn and Bip chose two large trees to cut back the outer bark to get at the inner fibers. They would only take small sections from each tree, replacing the bark to allow it to heal. Small scars from previous harvests could be found on all the grove trees. Bip pulled at the long sinuous fibers twice his size while Ryn shimmied up the trunk and used her sharp stone to cut them away from the top, then the bottom.

Mar and Par knew where to find the dye plants and lichen, it grew all around the grove. They moved slowly, stooping, picking, and stuffing the materials into carrying pouches. When the twins were farthest from the rabbit in his safe sleeping log and were efficiently pulling at a mound of grey lichen, Tich came to sniff at it. He let out a snot- spraying sneeze that made them laugh and push the cat away. "This one makes the green, this one colours it brown, and this leaf dyes the shum grey." Mar showed him her woven shum with its mottled hues.

Just then a wren swooped low over Tich, and he awkwardly whipped high into the air, just missing the small bird and landing with a heavy flop on too-big paws. Par laughed and Mar gasped at the comical chagrin on the bobcat's face, both the Crum shaking their green topped heads.

The Shum makers filled the baskets and tied them closed as the last rays stroked the highest treetops, pushing them in the rabbit's shelter to protect it further. The place the Crum always slept was a cleft between two large stones that was topped with a decaying log. They pushed out the larger branches and rearranged the leafy pile to make a soft nest, pulling their shums over their heads and bodies. The sleeping Crum looked like four little stones, blending easily into the foliage. Tich frowned at the curious balls before moving out of the grove for a bit of night hunting. The air cooled with the sun's descent, the moon took over, bright and glowing through the black tree silhouettes.

They were tying the straps of the baskets on their rabbit friend when the far grass parted and Tich called, "Greetings Crum!" Bip told the burden-ladened rabbit to hurry home to the burrow. "Stamp your feet if no one is around, someone will take these off you. Thank you for helping us!" He bowed low to the creature who warily looked aside at Tich before bounding quickly in the direction of the burrow.

The family had started after him, the cat trailing alongside, weaving a dodging the close leaves and trees, when the young cat ventured to ask, "Do you younglings want to try riding like Roo does on Fen?" Excited the twins pulled at their parents, batting their golden eyes, and trying to look adorable. "Ppleeese, Deda!" said Par. "Can we?" asked Mar.

"One at a time. "And "Take turns." they instructed; resistance was futile.

Ryn told Tich: "If they get too heavy tell them that's enough and let them get down."

"I'm first!" stepped up Par, tugging at the bob cat's leg. He squatted down to let her clamber on his shoulders. "Stay close. Don't go too far ahead." Bip called as the cat and passenger moved through the space between tree and bush, Par held on with two handfuls of long manes, getting used to the rolling motion, legs widely splayed. They were just starting to relax when a squirrel popped from behind a trunk, startling the cat who sprang straight into the air. Par had time the think, "Oh! Maggot-poop!" and tucked and rolled as she flew into a mouldy leaf pile. Unhurt but breathless, she threw an old leaf off her face and saw everyone laughing, especially Tich who was rolling around saying, "She said maggot-poop!"

Par and Mar took turns until the group reached the watch tree at the edge of Crum territory. Bip and Ryn had explained to Tich that all the animals within were safe from predators, adding, "That means you. But- you are welcome to visit if you are respectful of the other animals."

Tich watched the variously aged Crum climbing trees, riding animals, bringing in food that had been collected into the hole under the enormous oak and talking in dribs and drabs. It felt a little like a busy ant hill to the young and energetic cat, and with all those tasty looking meals hopping around that he wasn't allowed to eat. "I'll circle around your territory, scout out a good tree home." All four Crum bowed low to the bobcat, thanking him before he bounded away in great leaps.

CHAPTER TWO

FLIGHT OF CHANGE

Roo affectionately nose bumped and hugged Cra as she entered his families burrow room. They had been partners since last season after a small but beautiful ceremony held at the creek. Afterwards, Cra had moved from her mothers and brothers' smaller room into this larger one with Roo and his family. It was the workspace for Roo's mother, Cor, who was the clan leader and where his father, Hep, did all the finishing of the leather clothing he made. Roo's sister, Lyl, helped him with this when she wasn't flying on her owl or visiting South Burrow. Like Roo, the family's handsome heads were topped with waves and curls the colour of spring buds with luminous light green eyes. Cra shared Roos small alcove made close by the new double sized nest bed and although it was the largest of the family rooms in the burrow, it could feel crowded when everyone was home and working.

"How was it in Make-well today?" asked Cor as she got up from her desk with the new watch list that she had just made on the birch bark sheet.

"Fet is being looked after but we expect his passing soon, almost two-hundred years, he's ready. He's already picked his burial tree and the family are with him. I'll miss my old teacher." She looked melancholic and Cor placed a sympatric arm around her. Cor, almost as tall as Roo, was head and shoulders above the diminutive healer. "I'll look in on my way to put this list in the great hall." She walked into the burrow's main corridor, passing through the glow given from the niche of mushrooms that lit the hall.

Lyl took from the food shelf the large leaves the family ate from, and wooden cups for drinking the fruity tea. As the family ate crunchy chopped beetles over shredded dandelion leaves, they talked of all the day's happenings. Roo was his usual quiet self, letting the conversation fly over him and only dip into his head a little. He had been studying with several elders, absorbing their knowledge of the forest and its animals. Although he had had many experiences with survival, he wanted to become an expert on all animal traits. Roo harboured a grand and scary idea that he hadn't told anyone about- to start a new burrow to the north. Many years ago, his older brother, Jmy, had established South Burrow, moving with his partner and many others to live under an ancient beech tree. Tonight, he will whisper his thoughts to Cra before they slept, he needed to see if she was willing to leave her good work in the Make-Well, the place for healing both Crum and animal.

Bip stirred the long and heavy fibres in the specially prepared vat of water, oak Gaul, and other ingredients that they had been soaking in. This had made the fibres pliable for weaving and ready to accept the dyes. Ryn took one string at a time and dried them a little before weaving it onto the large circular loom. While the thick threads were twinned on the rods, the colouring leaves and lichens were placed intermittently to create the camouflaging pattern. It was Mar and Pars job to do this.

While the family worked in the alcove outside the clan pantry, Mir, Pip and Cra's mother, demonstrated to five young Crum the process of shum making. Mir moved to take over from Bip, then Ryn became the instructor, moving the young hands in a pattern through the tightly spaced loom rods. When all the strands had been transferred Bip released the water to drain. His part of the job was done for now, he could be free until his watch duty this evening. With a nose-bump to Ryn, winks to the twins and a smile to everyone else, he left the small alcove to go down the corridor to the main exit of the burrow.

Stepping out into the glorious noon sunshine, he surveyed the old forest, now replenished after the fire that had come through a few years ago. The stronger large trees had survived though still showing patches of burned bark, but cleaner now without the dead branches and messy detritus that goes with older sentinels. Small new trees, full now with shiny bright green had filled in the missing spaces. This part of the forest had a pleasant mix of the deep green conifers amongst the oaks and maples, with bushes of many varieties, much of them berry laden.

Bip walked through and around the full bushes and low plants of sweet fern that had replaced the explosion of flowers appearing after the burn. He was heading to the tall pine to visit with a great horned owl named Win, his flying friend of many years. Win made his nest just outside the Crum territory.

All around the wide trunk of Win's tree were the usual scatter of pellets and cones but Bip noticed new scratches in the bark as he climbed the tree. He was a short way up the trunk, finding his usual footholds and crevasses in the rough surface, When He heard: "Hello Bip! You found my new home!" It was Tich, draped on a fat low limb like a fur blanket, his spotted colouring blending perfectly with the bark.

"So, this is where you've ended up at, I'm on my way to visit with Win, I hope you are getting along." Replied Bip as he stopped to rest on Tich's branch.

"The old owl is up there; I hear him puffing and shuffling around. We were both hunting late into the night." The bob cat yawned hugely showing a fierce display of pointed teeth and a bright pink tongue.

"I'll let the younglings know where you are." Nodding to the cat he resumed the climb to the owl's roost.

The owl had an old nest in the tree trunk that started has a woodpecker's home until Win had kicked out the last bird. When the great horned owl faced out of the opening, his feathers of spotted browns and cream blended perfectly with the gnarly bark, only the round yellow eyes distinguished that there was a large raptor in the tree.

Win stepped out of his dark nesting hole and on to the lower branch at Bips call, snapping his beak and tilting his head to look at Bip. "How are you?" they asked each other at the same time. Laughing, Bip said, "I've escaped the shum-making for the afternoon and am on watch duty near here tonight. I thought I'd say hello in case you didn't see me while you hunted tonight."

"I'm feeling tired, I might be getting old, my friend." Huffed the owl.

Bip looked at the large golden eyes, still bright but noticing the bare patches of skin showing through the feathers. "Yes", thought Bip, I've known this owl for over twenty years. "It might be kinder to not ride on him anymore."

Win shook his great head, took a big breath, and fluffed out his feathers. "I can fly today, Bip! Shall we go now?"

With talons the size of curled rats, Win gripped the branch while Bip climbed on the lowered shoulders, well-practiced at setting himself to allow the free movement for Wins wings. He took a comfortable grip on the neck feathers. With an enormous sweep of wings pushing down air, they were air born, Bips heart was singing as always when they flew as the breeze flattened his hair and glowed his cheeks.

Mar and Par also had finished for the day, their places on the shum loom taken by the students. They exploded out the burrows main door and ran pell-mell straight to Tichs tree. Their father had never been told that they had discovered it's whereabouts earlier that week and had visited several times. Today they were to go riding for the first time since the shum gathering.

They had just reached the old pine when a high cry overhead was heard. Shockingly, they looked up to see their father in a free-fall, along with Win. The owl seemed senseless or dead, he and Bip were crashing through many branches and leaves. They could see their father as he flailed about, trying desperately to grab at anything, catching at leaves that stripped from branches, and falling, seemingly in slow motion. Finally, Crum and owl smashed into the centre of a holly bush. The twins cried out in horror and ran to the quivering bush as fast as they could.

The Watcher in a near-by tree who had witnessed it with disbelief and horror blew his warning pipe to alert the clan. As the many Crum ran towards him with spears, ready to deal with anything, the watcher called and pointed: "It's Bip and Win! In the Holly bush!"

Par was there first, Mar a step behind. Bip had landed on the owls outstretched wing, but Bips legs and arms were all at wrong angles obviously broken and some knocked or pulled out of joint sockets. It was terrible to behold. The owl had passed, eyes dull and half closed, the small bloody tongue sticking out from the open beak. Bip opened wide his mouth and eyes, suddenly gasping, pulling in the air that was smashed out of him. He moaned in pain. The healers came running- Cra and Mck from Make-Well. Mar and Par were pushed aside to make room for the adults, their shoulders touching, wide eyed and sobbing. Roo ran up to the two younglings and put his arms around their shoulders. "Come with me, we must tell Ryn and everyone else." With a last look over their shoulders they could see the healers moving Bip on to a make-shift stretcher. The twins were met at the burrow entrance by Cor and Ryn. "They are bringing him; he's breathing but hurt." Roo told them.

Bip was taken to the Make-Well room where they set his bones, put to right his joints, and wrapped the limbs with the healing moss and leaves that Roo and Cra had discovered a few years ago. But even with this, Bip was going to be there for a long time. Crum bones are hard to break but even harder to heal.

The Make-Well room had three tall nest beds built different than most Crum beds, higher and flatter, covered with leather and fresh grass leaves like all beds but at Make Well there were prop pillows made of fur and seed fluff and blankets of suede and fur. The rooms biggest feature was the large worktable surrounded by shelves of medicines in jars, baskets, and leather bottles. The other half of Make-Well was outdoors through the small door that led to a large landing. This is where the healers took care of the animals of the clan's territory.

Cra moved away from Bips nest-bed where she had been checking his bandages, to where Roo was standing by the door, staying out of the way. He watched as Bip was finally sleeping, surrounded by his family. Roo remembered when Hep was in that same bed recovering from injuries after a giant limb had fallen on him, the trauma of that awful time renewed. It was several years now and Hep could take watch duty now but infrequently.

Cra whispered to Roo, "We were going to tell everyone this evening. Shall we wait?" Roo nodded, as always feeling whole and centred when gazing at Cra, with her striking copper-coloured eyes and smooth fall of shiny hair the colour of fresh oak leaves. She looked up at her very tall partner and lovingly brushed the wild curls off his forehead.

"I talked to Pip about it, he loves the idea of the exploration north." Said Roo.

"We will speak our families tonight and pick a day that we can make the trip." He added.

"What if we took the twins with us? Said Cra. "It would allow Ryn to spend more time with Bip, and the younglings could use the distraction."

Roo gave her a crooked smile, "Are you sure, they can be a handful!"

"Eventually you are going to need to know how to handle a youngling!" Cra laughed at his wide-eyed look before gently pushing him out of the Make-Well room. "Go find Cor and Hep."

CHAPTER THREE

FINDING THE BURROW

The word of the trip north passed through the burrow like lightning. A few days after Bips fall the travellers for the exploratory trip were ready to leave. Roo and Cra would ride on Fen. Ryk, the raccoon friend of Pip's carried Pip and Par. Pip, stocky and easy-going, with straight unruly hair falling over his brow, was Roo's best friend and Cras brother. Mar took the first turn riding on Tich, the bob cat was wild with excitement and energy, moving ahead and all around the group on long gangly legs and too-big paws. Roo had made some strapping for around the chest and waist of the young cat, so Mar had some way to safely hold on to the too-mobile animal.

Two elders had joined the travellers riding on another raccoon, Ryks quiet and gentle mate, Ryh, Bry and Cin.

Bry had been in his youth, a hunter; hair almost white with dark green eyes, over one hundred and fifty years old but still strong and adventurous. He was excited to see again some of the old places he'd been to as a young Crum.

The other rider was Cin, she hadn't moved far from the burrow in her one-hundred and sixty-five years and wanted one last chance to see new places. As a fungi and lichen expert she would be a great help and Cra wanted to learn all she could from her.

Day broke with a cool mist whitewashing and softening all the foliage outlines as the group left Home Tree. All the animals but Tich bore small woven baskets with supplies and the Crum carried personal packs and pouches. Everyone but Mar had stone-tipped spears strapped across their backs. Although immensely proud to have her first spear, Par secretly wondered if she'd be able to stab at anything larger than an insect. They climbed onto their respective mounts and set off, first crossing the home creek then proceeding north along its bank. The pace was slow with the extra weight of two Crum passengers on the animals that usually carried one at a time. Behind Pip, Par was wide-eyed, her head on a swivel clutching at his waist, trying to take in every new plant and rock, while Mar was too busy trying to hold on and steady her young feline to look around much.

They followed along the creek's route north, a familiar trip for Roo and Pip who pointed out the features and landmarks as the day warmed: here was the poisonous lichen that Fen had got into: here was where Pip and Roo met the stag, Brn, again; and here was when Pip first met the young Ryk.

"I was just a little kit then!" Ryk remembered nostalgically.

"Yaa, look how you've grown- sideways!" teased Pip.

At the end of a long first day, they stopped at a hollow tree with the centre open to the sky. The animals were released from their burdens before they found various night perches on trees. The Crum pulled the baskets into the tree's interior. After a small meal of grubs and berries, they joined the baskets to curl into their shums to sleep.

Mar woke in the middle of the night to the screech of an owl hunting overhead. She watched as the bird's silhouette fleetingly blocked the stars. She shuddered, remembering again her Deda falling with the owl, Win, dead. Her whole body chilled at the thought of his near-death. She breathed deeply, pushing away the memory and let the cool air brushing her face and the warm smells from this new shelter with its thick humus calm her. She snuggled closer to Par. Tomorrow it was her sisters turn to ride on Tich. It had been so much fun but tomorrow she looked forward to enjoying the passing scenery behind Pip. Snoring softly beside her, Par clutched her new spear like a precious talisman, not dreaming at all.

Morning birdsong, dew dampened every surface: Cin slowly touched her fingers to her boots to stretch her sore back muscles. It was a wonderful trip yesterday, she loved Ryhs soft fur and her rolling gait, but Cin's lower half was totally unused to clutching the wide back of a raccoon with her legs splayed. Straightening she forgot the discomfort as the sun glowed on her wrinkled cheeks and she eyes rested on the sparkling creek as it shimmered and flowed over algae-smooth rocks.

Pip splashed water at Ryks snout as the raccoon drank. "Arrgh!" "Rat-head-Crum!" The big coon suddenly plopped into the creek, purposely coating Pip with creek-wave, then stood up to shake drops all over his friend.

"Flea infested-fish-breath-maggot-head!" They laughed and pelted each other. Cra, sitting on a half-rotted driftwood next to Roo, smiled at her brother's antics. "I don't think he'll ever grow up!" she mused.

Fen had finished the hunt for his morning meal and came to the creek for a drink, a safe distance up creek from the commotion. Tich joined him, still chewing and licking his muzzle. "How do you like having a rider?" asked the senior fox.

"The best part is the youngling's thoughts and laughs." The bob cat answered. "They are so different from us, fun and smart."

Fen nodded. "Sometimes Roo thinks too much, and I hear his darting ideas when all I want is quiet, but most of the time when we are hunting for the small rodents, him for the fur, me for the food, we are thinking about the same things."

Roo told the group at large, "We should reach the Great Falls later this morning. It's beautiful there. That is where we will make a base camp while we search for a good burrow and tree." He and Cra sat ready on the patient fox, ready to lead the party.

Par raced up to Tich as he obligingly stretched out his front legs, making his shoulders easily accessible. She carefully climbed up and followed Mar's instructions about the leather strapping to hold on to. Par leaned forward to hug his neck and scratch behind his ears. Grinning at them both and wiggling her brow knowingly at Tich, Mar told her sister: "Hold on!"

Bry held out an arm to Cin to help her get behind him on the female raccoon. "I bet you were sore from yesterday; I am too but at least it's pain that I remember from riding animals a long time ago."

Both the elders were now partnerless and had found an easy companionship in each other.

Pip and Mar said little as they rode on Ryk, the Crum totally engrossed in the amusing rambling raccoon thoughts as they followed the creek's edge north. They heard: "Look! Bird! I smell fish, yum. Frog! Jump- better not, Pip get mad. I hardly feel little Mar. Pip getting heavier. Baskets itchy. Ask Pip fix it. Smell great here. Go pee on it!" Pip and Mar giggled and waited for the raccoon to move away from the wet spot with a backward kick of dirt.

The land subtly changed as they neared the falls: steeper banks sloping to the creek, higher rolling hills, fewer deciduous trees.

Fen, Roo and Cra reached the falls first. They had been hearing its roar for a while and felt the moisture coating faces and fur. There were mostly conifers here with a few of the water-loving willows and thick clumps of tall reeds. At the creek head they could see the falls to the left feeding the large fast river to the right. The Great Falls were higher that the tallest trees, crashing down an escarpment of vertical rock. The Crum that had never seen the falls before were amazed and awed at both the crashing power of the wall of water, its bubbling foam at its base and the wide fast river. It's tributary, The Home Tree creek, seemed small and sedate in comparison.

Moving south along the wall, they made the short trek to the large leaning tree that had partly uprooted and fallen against the rock. It was a short way from the water, the sound here less overwhelming. The trees' few viable low-sweeping leafy boughs made a decent shelter against the wall. The animals were released to hunt and rest without baskets, the Crum asking them to check back with them at sundown and not to go too far.

After a simple lunch the Crum divided into groups to search in different directions. Roo, Cra and Cin wanted to explore around the water and would travel along the edge of the river.

Pip, Bry and the twins would go into the forest on the other side of the creek in search of the big "Mother Trees". Roo instructed before they parted at the water's edge: "The mission is to find a giant tree with its large roots raised from the earth or dug out to allow for the Crum to make a burrow under if one isn't already there. The tree must be healthy and the burrow preferably unoccupied!"

Pip and Bry kept their spears in hand as they moved into the cooling undergrowth, the surface angled riverward, working around fallen trunks and spindly new saplings struggling to get enough light to grow bigger. The birds were at rest or away now, the sounds of the afternoon forest had quieted to the rustlings of leaves made by squirrels and other rodents with interjection of the sharp ratty-rap of a unseen woodpecker. Par copied the older Crum and kept her spear at ready. They could see the mottled fur of Tich as he pounced on his lunch a short way uphill from them. Mar said hello to a startled black stripped chipmunk who darted away, frightened by the strange grey creature dressed in leather. They veered away from a hollow dip with its smell of skunk as they went from big tree to bigger tree, circling them in search of holes at the trunks. The sun began its western slant. As they wove through the brush, Bry told them of his exploits in this area almost one hundred years ago. "I had a black fox friend named Dar, we hunted here just like Roo does on Fen. One day a hawk dove at us, knocking me to the ground. I never knew what hit me until I heard its sharp scream. We didn't know its nest was just here." Bry pointed up at an old cedar, bare of fresh green and ready to fall over. Pip looked at the dying tree. The evolution of life had always fascinated him. Even now he could see all around the old grandfather there were young seedlings sprouting new life.

As they scaled over and around huge stones Pip talked of the bear that he and Roo had met above the falls. "I wonder if we will see him, if he travels below the falls." They laughed as he replayed the story of how they froze in place, trying to look like, "grey sticks" to fool the large omnivore.

They came to a small stream falling down their hill, making its bright way through clefts in stone and around trunks on its way to the river. A sun ray cut through the boughs overhead to make stars sparkle on the rapid flow. Glowing in the suns beam were several clumps of snowy Calla lilies nestled in the rust-coloured needles between the rocks. It was such a pretty place that they paused to enjoy the site until the sun moved, darkening again the dense surrounds. In view of the lilies there was a natural den made between stone with a thick roof made of lichen coated branches. Pip thought it was worth telling Roo about and maybe a place for them tonight.

Cin and Cra gingerly touched the scarlet and spotted toadstools and discussed their medicinal properties while Roo kept watch. The land near the river sloped steeply, all things attracted to its influence. They had been staying above the high bank, moving eastward the same direction as the fast water. Fen came towards them, slipping through trees, the sun spotting his fur with flashes of bright red, to join Roo's group.

"There is a burrow further upriver, but a wolverine lives there. "He told them, sniffing at the toadstools. They followed the fox, making their way over rocks and through trunks until they came to a small waterfall, the water coming through fissures from higher elevation. Fen told them to wait there. "I can smell him, but I don't see him."

Suddenly, a low snarl came from a huge old hemlock near the edge of the riverbank. A sudden burst of black from the tree had them scattering. Fen disappeared in an instant the other way. The Crum ran, grabbing at the nearest tree and scaling the rough bark high enough to escape the low-slung carnivore. Black and brown shot with grey, white muzzled, it a bull-dozed a path to their tree, smacked right into it and fell back. They felt the shudder and looked down with astonishment at the waving legs, looking so much like an upturned turtle. After a few minutes the wolverines snapping and growling became gasps, Roo ventured, "Are you alright?" Still on its back he raised his head in the Crum's direction. "This is humiliating! I've terrorized this hill all my life and now I can hardly see or move!" He panted and grumbled.

Huffing and heaving loudly, he twisted his nether half to force his body onto his bowed legs then stood swaying. He appeared very old looking, thin and bony, but Roo had never met a wolverine before.

Curiosity had Roo blurting, "How old are you?"

"Impertinent squirrel!" he growled. They saw that he couldn't locate them and kept moving his head, searching for them as they hung on the trunk just above him, notched toes, and hands into bark. His eyes were cloudy grey to match his face, his too-long talons cracked.

"We are Crum, looking for a burrow to make a new home in. But we won't bother you anymore."

"I'm hungry. Are you food?"

"No!" laughed Roo. Cra and Cin giggled. Cra said, "If you let us get down, we can find our fox friend and he might bring you something."

"Huh. I can't hunt anymore, been scratching at worms."

The Crum descended and Roo left to find Fen. The fox wasn't far, up another tree, grinning a shame-faced toothy smile. Fen nodded at the request and set off. "I will find Tich to help but we will throw the mice at him! I don't trust the miserable creature."

The wolverine waddled back to his burrow with the Crum following at a distance, the old fellow smelled terrible.

His burrow was the most curious and interesting that they had ever seen. A giant Hemlock draped it roots over the slope of a huge stone, hugging the low bank, imbedding in the soil both in the earth above and into the ferny patch at the rock base. In between the roots and rock was a burrow entrance, low and wide, well-polished from the oils and fur of the many years of wolverine passage. The short trek had tired the animal and he lay panting at the black hole.

There was a good-sized landing that lay between the small waterfall and burrow. The Crum saw the potential of this perfect setting, it would make a small but good Crum home. It was too bad it was taken, and how would they get rid of the smell? They climbed above and around the tree, noting it's good health and abundance of seed cones. A good crop of giant tree snails dotted its wood surface with many empty shells sitting on the ground.

Cra sat above the old fella on the upper roots and explained how they could talk to him, what the Crum were and where they lived. Soon they were joined by the rest of the group, Fen had found them up the hill, above this very stream. Tich, Fen and Ryk threw a few rodents and fish at the wolverine then retreated up the hill.

When the wolverine was full and sleeping, the Crum climbed up to the lilies. They ate some of the smaller snails, plucking the tender meat out of the shells and washed it down with the sweet stream water. They checked out the small den before the subject of the wolverine and his burrow filled their thoughts.

"It's perfect," said Pip, "Only one problem."

"Yes, it's unkind to even think of asking for his burrow. We could promise to look after him like we did that old porcupine until he passes." Roo said, referring to a dying friend that Pip had taken care of.

"I'm sure that if we left here and he dies, other animals will be quick to move into the burrow before we could get back. "Shrugged Pip.

"I like it here!" Mar exclaimed. The twins had been quiet during this whole episode, deferring to the adults. Par nodded, "It's so different from Home Tree, wilder, with lots of evergreens."

Bry asked, "Do you think you could find enough food here, other than pine nuts, fish, and snails?

Cin answered him, looking at everyone, "We found many edible plants and fungi, they are just different from what you are used to. There are plentiful of the medicinal mushrooms too".

Tich, who had wandered away chasing a moth, came leaping back, calling, "Come quick, he's in trouble!"

At the river's edge the wolverine was struggling to get out of the water. Before they could reach him, they saw his eyes roll up into his head, lifeless. He was swept under and away.

"I think he was wanting to wash or something." Sighed Tich.

"He sure needed it." Ryk said succinctly.

"Well, that's convenient." Said Pip, earning a swat from his sister.

"Should I try to follow his body?" Ryk asked everyone. They shook their heads. "This river is deep and fast. If we find him later, we can bury the body with respect but for now, I'd like to see this burrow!"

Roo, feeling slightly ashamed but eager, led them into the burrow. Hit with a blast o musky stench, the Crum covered their snouts with their shums.

Their animal friends inspected the exterior, peeing at the hemlock roots above to mark this place as theirs instead of the wolverines.

Roo asked to no one in particular: "It's weird how the roots are top and bottom, though I've seen that at home near our cave in the rocky hills, but how was this burrow made so big with the bank here?

"Maybe a small animal started digging it out first and then bigger and bigger critters until the wolverine. That way the tree could adjust and stay healthy." answered Pip. Roo took a moment to touch the trunk and feel the force of sap flowing under its bark. He laid his cheek against it and silently asked its permission, feeling the giving nature of this great tree.

CHAPTER FOUR

THE CLEANUP AND THE BEAR

The low entrance was just tall enough for Roo but much wider. Inside the ceiling was higher and the musky smell stronger, especially in the circular alcove that had been his sleeping nest.

A few large roots spiked down to break up the burrow and Roo could visualize how they would make anchors for the room dividing walls: the main corridor along the stone wall, the one great room and several others for sleeping and a pantry. "It's enough for no more than twenty or so Crum, and its good we have the lily den, but it wouldn't hurt to keep looking for another small shelter close by." Stated Roo.

Cra said she knows where some soap root plants are, and Cin added that her and the twins would collect a lot of leafy moss to scrub with. Before they left, however Par had been poking her spear into the back wall, "I think there could be an opening here, the soil between the roots and rock is thin." She knocked out a hole and a tiny bit of sun and fresh air came in.

"It would be great to have a crossflow of air." She poked her face at the opening and took a grateful breath.

Bry and Pip said they would start making the entrance much smaller. With size it was now they would have trouble keeping out other animals the same size as the previous occupant. Everyone got to work. They carried the largest stones they could find from the river edge and piled them at the landing, along with wood planks crudely cut from downed branches to make a door. Mixing chopped soap root and water in the giant snail shells, they began scrubbing the surfaces of wood and stone, careful not to disturb the good soil feeding the smaller roots of the tree. (This would be carefully walled off) Bry teased the twins that they were working harder here without any grousing than they ever did at home. The scent became more tolerable with the cleaning and airing although Cra said wryly that it was more likely that they were just getting used to it.

Late in the afternoon the exhausted group sat near the waterfall, on the piled stones yet to be used on the entrance hole. From there they had a clear view to the river. The sunset sky was beautiful, painted with cream and rose-gold that was repeated on the waters glassy surface.

They passed around a meal of dried currents and crickets washed down with the fresh water from handy waterfall caught in small shells.

Cin, thinking aloud, said' "It wouldn't hurt to bring back seeds from our berry bushes and plant them here."

After a moment, Roo said, "Before we go home, I think Pip and I should climb the escarpment tree again to see if the bear is still around. We need to tell him that there will be Crum establishing a place here. Also, he would know a lot about the animals in the area."

With the smell a little too strong still, the Crum secured the openings of the burrow with small stones and wood after they had pushed in the storage baskets. They retired to the sheltering den they had found by the lilies, pushing out a curious mole and much of the old leaves. As Ryk and Ryh climbed up into a tree above them, Pip joked that they had better not drop anything down on them: Ryk replied only with wink and a toothy grin.

Tich and Fen would find their own perches or holes after hunting.

The seven shum-covered Crum slept in a close pile, the tinkling of gentle water flowing close by at the crevice was music for their sleep. When Fen looked in at them, he thought they looked very much like a bird's stored collection of stones.

In the morning they found some small, attempted excavations into the burrow. The day promised to be another glorious sunny one. They uncovered the openings, hauled out the baskets and prepared for another workday of cleaning, plus the dirt floor needed to be made even. This involved levelling it with the filling of the dips with fresh soil and hard packing it down in preparation for a stone paving. Pip and Roo grinned and said how sorry they were not to be there to help but, gee golly, they had to look for a bear. They made a hasty exit as they were booed and pelted with dirt.

The two raccoons wanted to go to the falls also, so Pip and Roo accepted their fast transport. Ryk expressed the desire to see if any other raccoons were about and the fishing at the home creek tributary was easier. At the pounding rush of the Great falls they parted, Roo and Pip to climb the tall leaning pine to its very top, just under the lip of the rock shelf. In the few years since they had been there a curtain of vines had grown down from above, creating a handy drape to climb. Standing on top at the edge of the escarpment they looked at the river quietly passing before disappearing with its dramatic drop.

The two Crum retraced the route taken last time they were there, moving upriver, over and around boulders as large as them or bigger. They noted the changes the seasons had wrought, the biggest was the toppling of a balsam fir on to the rocks on either bank, now making a bridge crossing the river from side to side. Close to them was the huge root ball, most of its dirt washed away, looking like a giant multi-legged spider towering over their heads. Crossing this log-bridge they paused to watch the smooth water disappear at the horizon as if the world ended there. The only visual help was the foliage on either side that curved down over the sides and the distant bright snake of the lower river.

Roo and Pip looked for any bear-sign and it was easy to find. Deep gouges in the soft bark of a trunk, fur caught in the rough bark on another, marking it as a favourite back-scratching post. Then there was the alarming smell of rotten meat and the chewed bones of a deer. The two Crum watched the flies circle and land but kept their distance. Wrinkling their snouts, they moved farther along the riverbank until they came to the rock scree where they had found Fen's salvation, a healing plant only growing there.

Coming towards them, the sun and shade making roving dots on its brown fur, a large bear moved, long clawed paws turning inward, a yowling grunt with every right step. Roo and Pip quickly climbed a tree just in case it wasn't their friend, Dub. When they could recognize the familiar face of umber fur around small black eyes, they called out to him. "Dub! How are you?!" The huge head swung around searching until he spotted them as they made their descent from the tree.

"It's the Crum guys! I no see you long time! Good you are here, I need help." He plopped on to his butt and stuck out a paw the size of a small rabbit. There was an angry red sore on the side of the big toe pad. A small hole oozed blood and fluid. Roo poked gingerly at the pad and Dub rumbled a grunt. Roo looked up at Dub, "Can you make it down the escarpment? My partner, Cra, is a healer. She will know all about what plants and things you need.

"More Crum! Okay, I know way, not far. Climb up." They ascended the thickly furred leg smelling strongly of bear, rotten meat, dirt, and berries. Holding on to handfuls of hair with legs spread but kneeling, Roo and Pip once more experienced the rambling view from a bear's back. Limping slightly with each step, Dub moved quickly away from the river, through an aspen grove, covering vast tracts of forest, always moving southeast. The land began to slope downwards gradually. The bear made his way in a zigzag, always down, until he could shamble down a low rock fall. They were now level with the lower river.

"We have made a burrow where a wolverine had lived." They told him.

"He dead?! That mean old guy kept me away from there all these years. He fearless, bite at my legs."

"He died and fell in the river; we've been cleaning out the burrow for us."

"You coming here! Yah, I'm happy!"

"But please, Dub, don't scare or eat our friends: a fox, two raccoon and a bobcat."

"Okay, although I think raccoon don't taste too bad."

Pip said, "Please Dub, He's my best friend next to Roo."

Dub vibrated a rumbling laugh. "I no eat Pips friend."

They arrived at the other side of the river around noon. The bear didn't hesitate but ploughed straight into the strong flow, swimming across to the other side. Roo and Pip had to cling to the fur as the water had lapped up to their chests before the bear found footing on the shore rocks under the water.

No one was in sight, animal, and Crum both had hid at the site of a bear, not knowing if it was friend or foe. Dub shook, forgetting his passengers and Pip and Roo flew off him, tumbling back into the water, thankfully at the edge.

Dub cheerfully said, "Oops!"

Quickly going to the burrow, they called out that it was okay to come out. The twins came first, amazed at the huge wet mound grinning at them. Dub, in turn was thrilled to see matching Crum younglings. He laughed and made a pounding hop with his front paws, making them all back away.

Roo took Cras hand and hurriedly explained why the bear had come. Again, Dub plopped down and held out a dirty paw. Cra looked closely, touching carefully and smelling for infection. The bear watched her "smooth-like-a-new-leaf" hair and copper flashing eyes.

"Dub, I think you have a thorn stuck in your paw pad. It must come out or it will only get worse. We are not strong enough to hold you down. Can you hold still while I get it out?"

"I try." He told her.

"I have to get a few things." She said and ran back inside the burrow for her backpack. She always carried some basic medicines and tools just in case. "But I've never had this big of a patient!" Cra thought.

Pip helped with snail shells of water to wash the paw. Roo and Pip were to hold the talons apart so Cra could have better access to the wound.

"Hey, Dub, just don't get excited and throw us or we might never be found again." Roo said, only half joking.

"Kay, I like your Cra. She too good for you." Dub blinked and laughed, the rumble shaking his whole body.

"Be still, now." She ordered. Cra made a quick cut across the open sore and dove her hand into the widened opening. She felt for the thorn, clasped it and smoothly drew it out. At the hand going in all the on-lookers said, "Oh yuck and Eeewwwe!" Then Dub let out a howl that shook the trees and scattered birds, but he had kept his paw still. It felt better immediately. She hurriedly poured a cool infusion of black bark over and into the wound. "Can you stay off it for now, sleep here until tomorrow? Dub nodded, curled into a fur hillock, and was soon snoring.

Bry said, "We won't have to be worried about any animals taking our burrow while he is here."

They sat around what was now becoming the designated eating spot by the little waterfall. While they ate, Roo and Pip related their adventure and the route taken down from the height of the high waterfall to the river below, the others told of the cleaning and hauling of dirt and stones. Mar and Par sat together, faces grubby, clothing and boots covered with dirt. They couldn't stop looking at the breathing bear, so close. Bry said he'd never been past the falls, that the area that the bear had travelled would be good to explore sometime. Then he stood, stretching his sore back and they could hear his bones complain. "But not today!" he smiled.

Cin said, "This is the most physical work I've done in many seasons. Part of me feels young as these younglings and the rest of me feels very old!"

To the group in general, Roo stated, "I think you'd all agree that that's enough burrow work for the day. Tomorrow, I want to look for more wood that we will need in the forest, I'd like to meet more of the animals; some might start coming here now that the wolverine is gone, also, it would be good to get to know the trees and plants here, what could be used for the wood we need and more importantly, things that we can eat."

Although the smell was better in the burrow, no one was ready to spend the night there. They blocked up the entrance with large stones and wood again before they retired to the 'lily shelter', as they now called it.

They awoke to the crashing of rocks falling down the hillside and bonking on trees, making it rain leaves and sending birds to flight. Shaken with the calamity, they peaked out and saw Dub pulling great stones out of the ground and sending them downhill towards the new burrow. Before he could get out the next one out Roo ran out, waving his arms and yelling, "Stop! Dub! Stop! What are you doing?" The bear loped close, leaving talon stabs in the soft moss, and pushing bushes aside. "I see you try to close burrow with tiny sticks, I give you big new rocks!"

All the Crum were out now, looking at the path of destruction that the falling rocks had made. "Thank you, Dub, That's probably enough." Said Pip. The Crum moved down to the burrow tree with Dub following, happy to have helped. At the burrow entrance, the old barrier that the Crum had worked so hard on was now gone, scattered, and several stones, larger than a Crum was tall, were piled at the door.

"See!" He proudly said. Roo ruefully laughed, "Okay, can I ask you to move a few? Push this one close, here, and this one to the other side, and this one out of the way of the waterfall?" The bear easily nudged and swatted the rocks into place under Roos's instruction. They couldn't help but to look on in admiration at the once wolverine sized hole, now just wide enough to fit a Crum-made basket. Another rock was placed at the back of the burrow, obstructing entrance there to anything bigger than a standing Crum.

"Thank you, Dub, that's perfect. "Said Pip. Dub nodded once. "I go home now."

Turning, he bounded off the bank to the river below and slipped into the flow.

All they needed was to make a door, to wedge smaller stones against the tree roots and reclose the back hole. Roo thought that in time they could make a small roof over the two front entrance stones with wood and moss.

They would go home tomorrow.

Morning: overcast and dewy; every Crum energized with purpose.

Pip and the twins moved through the forest to call for Fen, Tich and the two raccoons. The baskets that had been tucked into the back of the burrow came out again and strapped on to Fen, Ryk and Ryn, now filled with snails and shells. Tich received his leather braces again. They closed entrances with stout and tightfitting wood backed by stone.

It started to rain on the trip back, a soft summer rain that had the Crum covering their heads with shums and tucking their snouts in to avoid a direct hit with the fat drops. The return journey was wet, slippery, quiet, and fast.

Par and Mars thoughts had turned to home, to their Deda, anxious to see how he was doing now.

Pip and Ryk were thinking of finding a quiet section on the big river and what they could catch there.

Cin was planning to start on the basket making the new burrow would need as she and Bry rode with the rolling gait of Ryh.

Bry was looking forward to his old nest-bed, all adventured-out for now.

Roos's mind was a darting mosaic of plans and ideas, excited in all the possibilities of the new burrow. Cra closed her eyes and laid her cheek against Roos back, her arms holding him close as they rode on the fox. She was happy and a little afraid. She would establish a new Make-Well at the North Burrow as the only healer. Crum couldn't read each other's thoughts, only the animals close to them, but she didn't need to hear Roo's, she could feel his distraction and eagerness.

CHAPTER FIVE

TO THE HOME TREE BURROW AND BACK

Bip was dreaming of flying on Win, soaring over the treetops, the noise of the wind shushing. Then the shushing was louder, followed by a hissing whisper:" Let him sleep!" He came awake, eyes fluttering to see three pair of beautiful golden eyes, the twins only a few inches from his face. They nuzzled and hugged, and he hugged them back as best he could with one arm, the other still held stiff with leave-wrapping.

Talking all at once, the twins ran over each other's words:

"You should have seen it!

"It's an amazing Burrow!"

"It had a wolverine!"

"It died!" (Half second pause of respect)

"Then we had to clean out the stink!"

"The bear helped us after we helped him."

"Wait, wait!" laughed Bip, and Ryn, anticipating his needs, came forward to nudge Mar out of the way and help him sit up. Cra came to his other side with a cup of water.

"It's wonderful to have you back and I want to hear about everything." said Bip, motioning the younglings close again. Mar and Par carefully crawled onto the Make-Well bed on either side, to huddle close. Ryn nose-bumped her family and said she'd come back later.

Hep and Lyl were chatting at the work benches as they worked on the leather clothing in the family's room. In their corner were shelves of stacked leather in various stages of becoming clothing and hanging from wall staves were the large, cured lengths of rat leather used for bed cloths. It made the burrow room fragrant and unique from all the other burrow rooms.

Roo had greeted them earlier and was now sitting on a stool next to Cor as she sat behind her paper covered desk near the family's room entrance. Pretty stones of many colours held down several piles, the curls of birch bark lifting at the corners. In a propped acorn shell were Cors assorted charcoal sticks and small quills. Outside the Home Tree they were having a blustery summer storm. They could hear gentle creaks overhead as the great old oak bent and swayed in the wind; the gurgles of rain as it channelled through and around the burrow on its way to the creek.

"On our next trip we'll bring seedlings of our edible plants to fill some of the holes made by Dub." Roo leaned forward in enthusiasm, telling Cor of his plans. She reflected that it was just this way when Jmy, Roo's older brother, was planning to move to South Burrow, taking thirty young Crum to establish a new home over ten seasons ago. And now Roo was wanting to do this too. She couldn't and wouldn't stop him or anyone that wanted to go but was cautious in her agreement - she was the clan leader, and the needs of the whole group would need to be met.

Seemingly to read her thoughts, Roo said, "I don't think we need many Crum to live there, it's a small burrow and we could come back here for some things like shums, clothing and berries."

Relieved, Cor said, "I'm happy you are thinking this way, I was worried that Home Tree would not have enough Crum left to defend it."

"It's different there, Mema, wild and rough. I think we will need fewer Watchers in the trees. At first, we will have to concentrate on making walls, floors, nests and things. We could make the Lily shelter more permanent and look for other shelters nearby. But they wouldn't be very defendable, maybe I need more animal friends..." Roo's eyes unfocused, plans being made at he talked.

"Roo, you will work it all out and I only ask that you take it slow, don't take too many Crum away from Home Tree and think carefully about how you want this new burrow to work. I'm happy for you, I'd hate to have you as well as Jmy so far away, not to mention our talented Healer." She smiled and lifted the list made on birch paper from the desktop. "In the meantime, with Bip laid up, I need you to take more Watches, starting tomorrow."

He laughed and left the families room, going to the great common room where several Crum were waiting out the storm, talking and playing games. A good storyteller, Roo was soon talking about his trip north, the wolverine and the bear. Many of the younger Crum listened, eager-eyed with the adventure of it and some asked more relevant questions, indicating a serious intention to go with him.

A few weeks later Roo was ready for another trip north. He had assembled a working team, everyone that could be spared that had the skills to cut and shape wood, set floors, and plant the future menu.

Pip and Ryk were happy to come, ready to find new fishing in the big river, Ryh was going to be with Ryk.

Fen said he would welcome the change in diet, there were more rodents in those hills.

Tich, too was happy to join them. He had grown in the short time they had known him, fuller and more powerful in his short body. When asked if he minded no riders but to carry baskets, he hesitated until he heard that Mar and Par would walk with him.

The Crum would be on foot, the two raccoons, the fox and the bobcat had to carry baskets full of the needed tools, leathers, furs, buckets, bowls, mushrooms, and plants. Tich wiggled and chased his bobbed tail until Fen told him to stop that, you'll get used to it. "Plus, they will be empty coming back, they might even leave yours behind."

Cra came of course to be with Roo but also as the needed healer just in case someone got hurt. She planned on collecting fungi and plants on the walk, something she couldn't do on the fast rides coming and going on the last trip.

Cin and Bry, promising to keep an eye on the twins again, accepted gifts of new shums from Ryn.

Along with the old group were three young, strong Crum: Lis, Til and Tym. Lis was short and thick for a female, with dark brown eyes and small green curls over a square shaped face. Til was the older brother to Tym. Both brothers had light spiky hair and matching soft brown eyes, only Til was slightly taller. The three had been working with wood and stone for all their forty plus years.

Everyone carried heavy packs and spears, even Mar. The animals, laden with filled baskets went ahead of the Crum to set the pace and warn of any other animals. Roo had instructed the younger Crum to be aware of their surroundings, not to depend on the animals' warnings. "We will be entering land, this time on foot, that has seen only a few passing Crum. Bry, Pip and I have our watch pipes, we hope to be able to use them in time, to make the aggressive animals leave." This dampened down any frivolity they might have shown but didn't stop the excitement.

The animals set a quick pace, the Crum following with Pip and Bry in front, the rest in the centre and Roo and Cra in back.

A barred owl crossed over them in the mornings grey sky, it was Lyl flying on the owl, Pon, waving. The creek they walked beside was blanketed with a thick miasma of fog, it's moisture coating everything it touched.

That night they stopped again at the hollow tree, taking the burdens off the animals so they could eat and recuperate. The Crum had a meal of freshly dug and washed grubs with small river snails. Cin had found a thorny blueberry bush and the berries finished the simple meal. "We will have to remember these for future trips." Cra said as she bit into a fruit the size of her palm.

"That's if Ryk and Ryn leave any." Said her brother. The two raccoons had stayed at the bushes, gobbling mouthfuls, careless of the spiney branches.

The morning was drizzly, fur and hair glistened with beads. Cra, Cin and the twins carried widespread mushroom caps to keep off the fine droplets. Laughing at their own cleverness, occasionally trading hands holding spears and mushroom stems. The rest had pulled their shums up, the land became hilly as they came closer to the creek's source, the surface full of rounded boulders and pine trunks, water-loving moss coating the gnarly roots.

The Crum had just begun a climb on a root covered mound when the raccoons above them screamed. A black wolf had Ryhs neck in its jaws, vigorously shaking the poor creature, basket straps broke, and they flew off. Bry was first to blow his Watch pipe, the piercing whistle hurting every animal's ear, but the wolf was gone before anyone could even throw a spear.

Shocked, Cin held the twins, all three crying. Ryk stood trembling with Pip who comforted him as best he could. Roo stopped Tich from going after the wolf. "It was alone, that's good for us. I don't know what we could have done if there was a pack." They divided the goods from the one broken basket amongst them to be carried, the intact basket was pushed under a jutting rock with boughs laid across it until they could come back for it.

The stunned and quiet travellers reach the new burrow without further trouble. They released Fen, Tich and Ryk, telling them to be careful, now, the wolf has found food with us, and it might be back. Roo asked Pip to take a first Watch duty on the Burrow tree while he opened the entrance a gave instructions. The first thing brought into the new burrow were the glowing phosphorescent mushrooms that would be established on the root walls. The Crum divided into stone haulers and wall builders. Roo took the next watch, allowing Pip to rest after the long day of travel and stress. The losing of Ryks companion showed on Pips grey face.

That evening the tired Crum sat around the seating stones, now arranged in two rough arcs to allow a perfect view over the drop-off to the river. The setting sun a low gold orb, visible through dispersing clouds. It repeated its light in the undulations on the rivers moving surface.

They slept that night, secure in the new burrow on piles of fresh grasses covered with skins of fur. Cra took the night watch duty. She was used to long shifts at Make-Well and was enjoying the night's song. The flying hunters blocked the stars as they sailed, the trees creaked and settled into the earth and branches swayed, rubbing with the light breeze. Pip joined her at dawn on the branch overlooking the steep and rocky forest. "How was your night?" he asked his big sister.

"A little cold but very fascinating. I watched Fen and Tich patrolling, they are happy with the food abundance here. I think Ryk was in that tree, she pointed lower on the incline. Pip nodded, "He's at the river now, washing his breakfast of a small snake."

Cra chuckled and stretched her arms overhead. "I'm sore from placing rocks into dirt floor."

Pip said, kindly' "It's going to be noisy in the burrow, maybe you could sleep in the lily den this morning."

"Good idea!" She patted her brother's arm, passed him the watch pipe, and climbed down the hemlock's trunk.

Roo hugged her one handed when she stepped down on the tree's upper roots, holding two bundles of food. They climbed to the lilies to eat, sitting on the soft moss outside the shelter. The water's tinkle couldn't compete with a million newly awaken birds rejoicing above them.

Cra sighed, her gaze on the velvety snow-white blooms touched by a slanting beam.

While she slept, Roo moved uphill over the needle-strewn rocks, seeking for animal sign and potential resources. One of the huge holes left by the bear's good deed had exposed a vein of white stone. Touching it and licking his finger, Roo tasted salt. Green eyes widened at this precious find, he thought of his father's leather work and all the other uses of this mineral. He took several large stones to cover and protect the salt from washing away with any rain. They would have to take some home in a basket. His mind went to poor Ryh and the wolf, then to the basket that Fen and he had retrieved full of needed goods.

Carrying a large chunk of a fallen branch to the burrow, Roo checked on the progress of his hard-working friends while they took a meal break at the seating stones. The floor of the whole burrow had been laid with smooth flat river stones, the rocks multi-coloured and fitting close. Wall dividers had been made going from the stanchion pillar roots to the far wall of thicker roots and dirt. This back wall was now planked with new panels with only the mushroom niches cut out. New crops of the glowing fungi had been placed in the dirt niches, tamped in with moist moss. They even had made a wonderful heavy wood door for the entrance, cleverly balanced to swing easily. What was needed now was the finishing: the round nest beds fashioned from wood and leather, shelves and furniture made. Before that, they needed a break.

Smiling, Roo went to the grubby bunch of Crum. It's wonderful! No more work today." Mar and Par grinned at each other. They wanted to find Tich and explore the forest. "No one is to be alone, the younger especially. Roo looked sternly at Lis and the brothers, then at the twins. "And don't go far, stay in site of this tree." He pointed at a very wide and tall sycamore that could be seen from a good way.

Pip went with Lis, Tym and Til while Cin decided to stay close to the burrow, her break time better served by resting her old muscles.

Bry said he'd stay with Mar and Par and Roo said he'd stay here, that Cra would wake soon.

The first thing they all did was wash at the waterfall next to the burrow. The day was very warm now, the cloudless sky a clear robin's egg blue.

Pip took his charges along the riverbank, past the curve where most of the burrow floor stones had come from. He was looking into the clear water for natural platforms that he could fish from. They found secluded shallow eddies where plentiful schools of minnows had found sanctuary out of the strong current. Lis squatted to watch a green crab the size of her hand as it jittered sideways into the water. Tym skipped a stone that reached almost to the other shore, startling a great heron into flight. Til, spear in hand and pipe ready, kept a look-out on the forest above them.

From a rotting log a parade of puff-ball mushrooms sprouted, the largest was bigger than Par's head. It proved to be too much of a temptation, and she ran at them, smashed the largest with her hands and with a gleeful scream, hopped away from the explosive cloud of spores. Mar ran squealing after her while Bry covered his snout with his shum and followed, shaking his head.

Mar was inspecting a small snail when she heard a caw and felt the swoosh of wings. A crow set down near her and pecked at another larger snail clinging to a fallen limb. "Oh!" she gasped in surprise. Crows were very intelligent but hardly ever had anything to do with Crum. Apparently this one was different. "Hello!" The crow said. Par, not far away, had stopped moving at this, suspending her poking at a beetle with her spear. She bent quickly and tossed the beetle in a gentle arc to the crow who caught and swallowed it whole. "Thanks! I've seen you. You are Crum." It spoke.

Mar smiled, "I am Mar, and this is my sister, Par." Quick as lightning, stabbing with its beak, it speared the snail, breaking it open to get the meat inside. "Eewwee." They grinned. "I am Acky. I saw the end of that miserable wolverine. Are you going to stay in his burrow now?"

"Some of us will stay, Roo wants to make this another burrow where he can learn the ways of all the animals so he can teach all the Crum." Par answered. Bry listened to the exchange from nearby, coming closer, he said, "I am Bry. I know that Roo would like to meet you. If you come near the wolverine tree you will see him, he's taller than any of us." The crow turned his ruffled head and took off, calling, "I'll tell the birds!" The trio was delighted with meeting the friendly crow.

Tich landed with a startling thump next to them laughing as they jumped. "We are touring the forest, is there anything good to see.?" Asked Par.

"I've been scaring a lot of mice and a few chipmunks." He grinned, all toothy fangs and hazel eyes shining. "Cave up there. It's a bit batty." They followed the bobcat's stubby tail up the hill.

Cra found Roo planning curls of wood shavings off a large plank balanced on two rocks. "I've given the workers a rest day, you too if you want to go. I'm staying to do small jobs like this." As he spoke, Fen joined them, curled into a red fur ball and closed his eyes. Not looking at them they heard him say, "So much food! This place is paradise."

Cra chuckled, "But not Crum food." I see Cin by that spruce, I'll go food hunting with her."

Fen slitted open an eye at Roo. "There is a cave up the hill, I think Bry is going with Tich and the twins to find it."

"What's it like? The same as our cave at home?"

"No," he hesitantly answered, "In a hole. Bigger, with funny stone sticks coming down. Lots of bats live in it. Smells."

"Any animals other than bats?"

"Hum, not when I was there but I smelled some: the wolverine, other raccoons and foxes, small rodents. Most smells are old. Opening hole small, smaller than this." He nose-pointed to the burrow. I smell that wolf in the forest, I don't think he is far." cautioned Fen.

The plank was smooth now. Roo replaced it with another on the level stones and began again, quietly working while Fen snored softly.

CHAPTER SIX
THE WOLF AND THE CAVE

Cin and Cra had decided they needed baskets first before gathering much food. They had climbed a large willow and were cutting off the long thin stems that made great pliable weave for baskets. They were working halfway up the light grey tree, using stone knives to cut away every second of the reddish stems in order not to stress the tree. The long spear-leaved lengths fell to the ground in curling twists. The two Crum were carefully sitting on the bigger branch with their legs hugging it and one hand securely clamped on another smaller branch. They were almost done the cutting when the black wolf crossed under them, noticed the curious pile of branches, sniffed at the trunk, saying to himself, "There is that smell again. What is it?" He lifted his leg and squirted urine on the trunk. Cra and Cin wrinkled their snouts at this but were glad not to be discovered.

"He was going towards the burrow!" whispered Cra. They made their way down, leaving the willow pile and followed the wolf.

Pip found Ryk far away on the riverbank, scooping out crayfish from a pool. As they watched he started chewing them, one after another, all the while humming, thinking: "yummy! and, so good."

Lis grimaced saying, "Yuck!" and Til and Tym smiled with disgust and fascination as the fish drool flew from the raccoon's busy mouth.

"Have you seen the wolf?" Ryk asked of Pip. Ryk swallowed the last body, then licked his lips.

"No, but I think he's not done with us yet. Will you be okay here until we go home? I think we will be here a few days still."

Ryk nodded yes, "I plan on staying here at the river's edge, sleep in that big pine." He indicated a close tree.

"I know something must be done, maybe we can ask Dub to help somehow. He is a predator we need a bigger predator to make him leave us alone."

Tich guided them up to the cave entrance, it wasn't easy to find, they had to carefully climb down a steep crevice and then from its bottom, up the rock wall a short way to an opening no larger than a Crum. Telling them to wait at the bottom, Bry went first to peek into the angled entrance. The faint light revealed a few stalactites spearing from the ceiling, some of them broken by past visitors. A strong stink of bat guano made him turn his head back to take a breath. The uneven floor was heaped with the source of the smell along with a few leaves and some bones. A soft flutter came from above, dark grey shapes, half the size of a youngling, hung from the ceiling. Unfamiliar with bats and their ways, he said to himself, "No way I'm going in there!"

He told them what he had found and the twins each had a look, one at a time.

Par said' "Ooh!" loud enough to cause a stir with the occupants. Not satisfied with that, she hooted like an owl, causing several of the bats to stir awake. He said, "Let's get out of here!" and they all scaled the wall out of the crevice, Bry thinking he was getting too old for younglings' antics.

That night Roo was on watch above the hemlock burrow. He had his spear and pipe ready and his warmest shum covering both head and shoulders. A full moon sat over the horizon, the sky a deep purple-blue expanse behind the spiking black profiles of treetops. The moonlight made contrasts of light and shadows; soft blue cut with deep indigo. Movement caught Roo's attention. It was the wolf, dark and silent, slinking towards the burrow.

"Don't come closer. I'll blow this pipe; you've heard it before. Our animal friends are not here." The wolf searched the tree, but the Crum was invisible against the grey trunk.

"Hmmm." Said the wolf, casually sitting on his haunches and looking in Roo's direction. "The fox and bobcat are too fast to catch, but I smell the other raccoon. Where is he?" The wolf quietly menaced.

"Far away. Leave here or I'll make you leave." Roo told him.

"How? The bear doesn't come here, his territory is up there." He waved his head in the direction of the great waterfall and escarpment. Roo didn't answer.

"" Well, I must go hunting!" the wolf chuckled meanly, turned, and blended into the shadows.

Roo was worried now for Ryk and any other animal near this burrow. This wolf has decided to make this his territory. Travel for Ryk, especially, will be very dangerous; something had to be done.

A few hours later Roo was sitting on the cool hemlock branch, dangling his feet and watching the eastern edge glow a bright pink, the sounds of the birds making the usual morning symphony. Acky landed near him, cawing, "Good morning." Roo heard this in his head. They had met after Acky talked to Bry, the crow becoming a fast friend. Acky told Roo what was happening all around them, a very valuable asset.

"The wolf is down by the creek where he took your raccoon." The crow told him.

"Have you seen Dub, the bear?"

"No but I wasn't over the falls today."

"We will have a meeting this morning, all of us Crum and animals need to figure out how to get rid of the wolf. I'd value your ideas and letting us know the whereabouts of the wolf. Thank you, Acky." The crow nodded and pushed off the branch, shaking the hemlock needles.

Fen, Acky and Tich joined Ryk and the Crum at Ryk's tree, the tall pine that leaned towards the river. It was a good vantage point, and everyone felt safe there.

"What shall we do about the wolf?" he asked the assembly. "As long as he's here, we are not safe, and he'll eat Ryk when we try to go home.

"Let's not have that." Ryk succinctly said.

"" What if we get Dub to attack him, he's the largest predator here. I could go look for him." Said Pip.

Bry joined in, "I'd like to go with you."

"I wish there was another way than to kill him. Crum do not kill animals accept the mice, rats and voles we make our clothes from. Even then we are happy to ask Fen and others to do that for us." Roo added this for Acky's sake.

The crow told them: "He calls himself Zek. He was exiled out of his pack west of here. And he kills for the fun of it. He destroyed a whole family of rabbits but only ate two.

"Too bad we can't stuff him in that cave." Mused Lis.

"He wouldn't fit in the entrance." Said Mar

"But it's a deep crevasse... just how do we get him into it and how can we make him stay there?" asked Par.

The group all fell silent, all furiously thinking. Roo sighed and gazed unseeing at the forest above the bank, so alive and beautiful.

"Pip and Bry should seek out Dub and see if he can help. There is still work to do in the burrow and food to be gathered and stored. I need to plan and think on this, if any of you have any ideas come to me." He thanked the animals, and the Crum went up the bank and entered the woods again.

Are you able to make this trip? It's not an easy journey." Pip asked Bry. He looked over the older Crum with his white hair and knobby joints, but Bry had the heavy corded muscles of a youth and bright eager eyes.

"I wouldn't miss this! I haven't felt this young in many seasons even if my bones are old." Bry grinned happily. Both Crum carried light packs of food and tools along with their spears. Pip had one of the piercing watch pipes. They had left at mid-morning, moving quickly and quietly through the forest but always parallel to the river. They came to where the creek spit off south and climbed up a tall tree, looking out for the wolf. Acky swooped close to the Crum to tell them that the wolf was in the forest near the burrow. They climbed down quickly. Across the creek and past the wide-open area and into the low bushes on the way to the falls. The rumbling roar enveloped them as they pushed out of the leaves. The great falls: a wall of white, all sparkling with iridescent pinpoints of stars. The mist coated face and hair, Brys hair became curlier while Pips flopped down over one eye.

At the leaning tree, Pip and Bry were thankful that it was still leaning. One day it would topple, and they would have to find another way up the steep cliff.

At the top, a breathless Bry bent to catch his breath. Pip looked around, the river sedately falling away from this height, hemmed with boulders and deadwood. The trees here much like the type down below with the occasional white birch to break the green vista.

"Not much new bear sign." Commented Pip as he checked a scratched tree. Drops of old sticky sap had dried in the bark's furrows. They crossed the river on the new tree bridge without incident and met a sleek brown muskrat as he slipped glistening out of the river, clutching a fish.

Bry asked if it had seen the bear, where he might be now. "Not many days I no see. Maybe gone hunting." With a blink he re-entered the water, small head carrying its meal of fish cutting vees in the surface.

Pip led Bry to the stone scree where they ate and rested. He plucked at a small plant and stuffed it into his pack explaining: "This is medicine, my sister might need more of it." It was a cure for the poisonous lichen. "Although I don't think Fen will ever make that mistake again."

"I think we should look around a little more, last time we were here, Dub came from that away." They followed the bears route into the aspen grove.

"When I was a young hunter, I never came here, the leaning tree was not there and only a few Crum had ever climbed the cliff." Bry said.

They were encompassed by the constant leafy shushing and twittering's in the grove. After a while they stopped to rest. They had a decision to make, there was still no sign of the bear. Should they keep looking or go back to their waiting friends. "A bear can cover a lot of forest in a single day. He needs to eat big so must find bigger animals, deer, elk or…or…" Bry hesitated, and Pip finished for him, "Raccoons. I know."

They went home. Across the river, down the tree, over the creek and into the forest, arriving after dusk at the burrow. Tym was on watch and seen the two exhausted Crum, Pip helping Bry the last of the way. Knowing that Roo was still awake and watching at the riverbank, he called down: "They are coming!"

Roo met them and helped get Bry into his newly made nest-bed. "No bear, no fresh sign, must be gone hunting." Whispered Pip. Roo nodded and directed Pip to another nest-bed before finding his own. They had beds for six, he and Cra shared, of course, and so did the twins and the brothers.

Tables and Chairs were still being made but the pantry shelves were in place and mostly full. Cin and Mar had been gathering and making baskets while Lis, with her student, Par, carved wood bowls and crates. The whole place smelled of fresh cut wood, clean earth and assorted fragrant leaves, all softly illuminated by the glow-shrooms.

"I've an idea but it's crazy." Said Roo. Bry was the last to stumble out of the burrow, squinting at the new day, even if the sky this morning was overcast. Cin handed him food balanced on a fresh leaf as he dropped heavily on to the stone seat.

Pip joined them, head dripping from the waterfall where he had held his face into the cold flow to shake off the fatigue. Cra gave him food and he lost no time, stuffing in large bites of walnuts alternating with berries. "You eat like a raccoon." She complained affectionately, a common remark she made to her brother.

"It will take luck and all of us- we need to trap him in the crevasse where the cave is." Roo looked at the Crum surrounding him. Fen was there with Tich, but Ryk was keeping safe back at his pine tree.

"It's very narrow and steep, I don't think he could jump or climb out once he is down there. I went to inspect it yesterday. We just need to get him to fall in somehow. Ryk would have to be the bait." At this Pip opened his mouth to protest and Roo held up his hand. "I think we can do this and keep him safe."

Cra said, "Can we cover over the hole, so it's camouflaged but not safe to step on?"

"Yes!" piped in Cin, excited, "We can use the long willow branches going across..." "And cover them with leaves and stuff!" finished Mar, smiling.

"The other forest animals must be warned not to go near there, or they will fall in." Fen looked at Tich who said he would tell them too.

Two mornings passed and the trap was ready. It took convincing and a very good plan to get Ryk back into the forest. First, Acky let Ryk know when it was safe to enter. To be aware of the wolves' movements was very important. Tich had led Ryk to the crevasse each day, asking him to urinate along the way at various spots up to the trap. Each night the wolf searched along the scented places.

On the final day Ryk took his place at the hole's lip, careful not to upset the leaf-covered branch ends.

"If I get eaten, I'll drown/bite/smack Pip!" mumbled Ryk, trying to look like a tempting grazing bunny.

Acky flew low, cawing, "He's coming."

The black wolf moved faster than they expected, darting up the hill in a direct line to the raccoon. Just before he jumped on the wide-eyed Ryk, everyone burst into action: Ryk fell fast to the side. Tich leaped from a tree to slam into the wolf. Fen burst from a side bush to push also. Roo blew the painful watch pipe. All the Crum thrust spears at the wolf. Snapping jaws and twisting, he almost didn't fall in, desperately scrabbling for purchase but finding only loose willow stems. A terrible cry of anger came from the hole that was cut short with an awful thud. Then silence.

Cra covered her face with her hands and buried it into Roo's shoulder as he leaned in to see. Pip was hugging Ryk, checking to see if he was okay. Cin stayed back, not wanting to look. She was sad and tired that it had come to this. The other Crum looked in. In his last twisting he had landed badly, his neck was at a severe angle. They were quiet and motionless until Fen came up to the hole and peed down into it. Cra gasped and laughed. Bry chuckled and wiped his brow.

Lis just shook her head. Mar, looking the longest, asked, "What will happen now?"

Roo told all of them: "His body will return to the earth, the animals will feed, the ground will be nourished. We will have peace here for a while until this territory is known to be protected by Crum. We need to make more animal friends here so we can help each other." Fen said after a second of silence: "Good speech."

Everyone descended through the woods. By the time they came close to the burrow they were chatting easily again.

The large fur hillock was back, Dub enjoying the sun's heat in the clearing. "Hi guys! You looking for me?"

CHAPTER SEVEN

FAMILY TIME

"You will spend the winter there?" asked Cor. She needn't have asked; she knew that this was Roo's responsibility and dream. All Crum hibernated over winters and the new burrow needed to be always occupied or animals would try to make it their home.

Roo nodded. "I've left Cin and Bry there for now and will be going back soon. We will find out soon who wants to over-winter there. Cra and I for sure but everyone else can choose how long they can stay. It's a small burrow, we can comfortably house only twenty or so all the time."

They were in the family's room at the eating table. Hep and Lyl had been listening quietly, letting the usually reticent Roo talk about the new and wild burrow. Cra was visiting with Bip, checking on his healing progress.

"I'd like to come when you go." Said Lyl, her green eyes flashing with eagerness.

"I think we should all make a visit while it's still summer. I want to see it." Added Cor.

"My work is good for now; I can leave it. I've been teaching young Pye to hunt, he has made a new friend of a young fox, one of Fen's many sons.

"That's great, Deda! There is a lot of small rodents in our hills, eventually we will be able to supply Home Tree with furs, and I found a wonderful new vein of salt. We brought you back some, it's at your workshop."

Cor asked, "When will you go? I can transfer my duties to Ryn now that Bip is better."

"Soon. Two weeks? I'll check with Cra on that, and I need to see who wants to come to stay a while."

Pip was in the creek, the top line of a net in hand, watching the small flashes of fish catch while pushing away the too large, sweeping them out or throwing them to Ryk. The raccoon was depressed but nipped off the trout's head anyway, muttering, "A coons gotta eat." Ryk had returned to the small den he had shared with Ryh, nosed about it, peed on the outside to re-mark it as his and then went to the creek.

"Sorry Ryk. I think we will be going back to the north burrow soon. Roo wants to know who will be going back with him, either as visitors or to stay. What do you think?" Pip pulled out the net of flipping silver, hauled it up the bank to dump the load into a waiting vat. He would drain most of the water before transporting it across his strong back to the clan's pantry.

"I want to go, to stay there; I won't ask you to stay if you don't want to." Said Pip.

"Food is better there." Ryk, cheering up, answered, "Sure!"

Bip was standing in his family's room, with his twins on either side of him, taking steps for Cra as she watched.

"Good! How's your arm?"

"It still hurts but I can use it now, just not to carry anything heavy yet."

"I'm so glad." She smiled at the family. "The twins will tell you all about our adventures, but I'll just say that they were wonderful, helpful and got along!"

Ryn rolled her eyes and laughed, so happy to have them back again and to have her partner doing so well.

Roo was on watch duty during the day, back on the branch of the tree that he liked overlooking the Home Tree creek and in sight of the Make-Well landing and his father's fur-curing shop. He received waves and hellos from the Crum to-ing and fro-ing all around the Crum burrow. At noon a crow descended on to his branch, it was Acky's friend reporting that all was well at the North Burrow. "Dub has been cruising by, making sure that no other wolves come near." Roo thanked him for this service, for coming all the way. "I didn't have to come so far; we passed the word along." The crow then swept off and away.

That evening Roo spent a little time in the large common room. In one corner a trio were having a small concert with pipes and a drum. The music began slowly with the tap-tapping of rain drops, flowing into wind and bird song, ending with a crescendo of water rush. Applause, stamping and banging on tables. The three musicians bowed low, grinning.

Roo joined Lis, Til, Tym and Pip at a table. The first thing he said was that he was going north again in a few weeks and that his family were coming for a visit. "I also want to ask who of you want to stay over winter."

Pip raised his hand, "Ryk and I, we love the fishing."

"We were just talking about that. "said Lis. "Tym and I would like to come."

Til told him, "I will stay here and help our parents, at least for this winter."

They were soon joined by most of the room's occupants and Roo told the story of the wolf while the others added the bits of their part. He made the tale light, making much of the Crum heroics, the truth of what he felt of the sad death he kept to himself.

Tich danced around, needing to get going, enough of all these goodbyes. A bushy red tail whipped across his nose. He stopped moving and sneezed twice. Fen's young daughter, Weh, laughed and jumped out of reach, upsetting her baskets. Fen lightly cuffed her. "Be still, we are going in a minute." Ryk stood apart, patient, thinking, "This large bunch are going to make a slow caravan." He gazed at the milling Crum, giving last minute instructions, goodbyes, and hugs.

Mar and Par looked on from the side of the creek, envious. They weren't going this time. The food-gathering work was waiting, and they were to begin their "watch" training.

Lis moved to Tich to again tighten his basket straps. She could feel the excited bobcat tremble with energy under the soft matt of grey-brown fur.

Roo called out to the assembly, "Ready?" Again, the animals led the way, but this time Fen and his daughter led the way. Ryk, then the Crum with Tich to follow in the rear. Roo thought that this arrangement might make hungry predators think twice about the raccoon, a very round well-fed fur-ball.

"Protect the rear." Roo ordered Tich, and thought, "At least in the back he could hop around and not bother anyone."

Hep, Cor and Lyl joined Roo and Cra. Pip walked with Lis and Tym. Three more had joined the group with the intentions of staying over the winter: Mac and his partner, Kam, and Blu. All were middle aged, around ninety years. Mac: short, strong, short haired and skilled in all trades. Kam: slim, long light grey-green hair, former hunter, now a musician and watch-trained. Blu: round and solid, short stubby hair, a skilled carver and stone worker.

The mornings fog had burned away when they finally set out. Lyl knew most of the way from above, but her owl didn't travel as far north as the great falls. When she took long flights, it was always to South Burrow. She planned on revealing to her family on this trip that she would be wintering there with her brother and her sweet Gyn, soon to be her partner. That would leave Mema and Deda alone in that large burrow room. On impulse she hugged her father's waist as they walked. Hep laughed and squeezed her shoulder. She blurted: "I have something to tell you, Deda." Over hearing this, Cor turned to her and smiled, "Are you going to say that you and Gyn will be partners now and that you are going to move to South Burrow?"

"I've been obvious, I guess. "

Roo hugged his sister, "Finally. We wondered if you'd ever get around to it."

"But the big family room?"

They all knew that space in the burrow was limited. With Roo, Jym and now Lyl going, a change would have to be made.

"I'm going to ask Bip to become leader, they can bring the shum-making in that room, we would trade places. Hep's leather working will fit where the twin's alcove is." Cor told them.

"What will you do with yourself?" asked Roo, "Now that you won't be ordering us around?"

She smiled at him, her face suddenly carefree. "I want to hunt again." At their surprised faces she told them how she wanted to be outdoors more often, that maybe she could find another animal like Fen who will do the killing for me." Tich was listening to this conversation, as always fascinated with Crum thinking. "Ask Weh! She said she'd like to be a hunter like Fen."

Cor turned to the bright hazel eyed cat and nodded. "We can try a few rides when we are settled at North Burrow." She bopped his pink nose and patted a tufted jowl.

"I think Bip would be a good leader, after all he had to raise those twins!" said Roo, making them all laugh.

As they approached the hollow tree for their overnight rest, they found it occupied with a large brood of possums. Mother possum was not pleased to see the foxes and bobcat and hissed wildly from the entrance. They lost no time in backing away. Pip remembered a huge, uprooted tree further off their path. They hurried to it, wanting to be secure before full dark when the night hunters were out. It was in amongst the enormous scraggly roots that they pushed and snugged into. It wasn't perfect, but they took the baskets off the animals and left them to find their meals and night perches in the trees.

With the fading magenta sky purpling, they passed around a simple meal of grubs wrapped in grape leaves and drinks of sweet cool strawberry juice. Before finally curling into the shums, they pulled an insulating layer of leaves over them, making the Crum invisible to any creature.

Cor woke to a tickling on her snout. Startled she brushed away a finger-sized curious ant and quickly stood, shaking off several others. Everyone got up at once, shedding the visitors and knocking off many that coated the baskets. "It's been many years since I've slept out of doors, I forgot how much fun it could be." She said with a little grumpiness.

A quick wash at the creek and the travellers continued the last part of the trip north. Never tiring of the view and wanting to share it, Roo detoured to the Great Falls where they paused to witness it's power and beauty.

CHAPTER EIGHT

MEETING SOMEONE NEW

Bry "Hallo-ed them from his branch on the burrow tree, grinning, and waving: Cin stood up from her basket weaving set by entrance in the sunshine.

The newcomers were given the interior tour and dutifully oohed and aahed. The animals were released from their baskets and straps, all speedily made for the trees with the echoes of Crum thanks in their ears.

Bry and Cin set out a small feast, having heard from Acky that they were coming close. All the Crum enjoyed dining at the seating stones to watch a glorious sunset over the water.

While Bry and Cin were on their own they had made more sleeping nests, some only temporary, as it was a larger crowd now in the small burrow.

Roo thought that expansion was possible if they made the lily shelter more permanent and maybe in the far future, another level below the main one like it is at Home Tree.

Cor stated, eyes shining: "Tomorrow I'd like to take a ride on Weh to see if we could be hunting partners."

"If Fen is willing, I'd like to look further into the forest hills, meet more animals. With the setting up and the wolf, I haven't been able to see the whole hillside."

A perfect summer morning began with pretty much everyone scattering, only Cra and Cin stayed behind at the Burrow. Roo's only stipulation to the wanderers: This place is still wild, never go anywhere alone and take a watch pipe with every group."

Roo and Cor found the foxes looking into the wolf's crevasse where a disgusting smell of decay wafted up from the carcass, bones poking out of mangy fur.

"There is a bat cave down there, but I don't think I want to visit it this summer." Roo pulled his shum over his snout.

"Fen, I'd like to explore more of the forest and Mema wants to try riding on Weh. Are you both willing?"

The foxes squatted low. Weh copying her parent. Roo mounted easily; it was second nature after hunting together these many years. Cor was not as tall or heavy as her son, but Weh needed to learn how to move with the new weight, to not upend her passenger. Cor sat on the young foxes' shoulders, bent her knees back a little and held on to the soft red mane. "Just a few steps first, okay, Weh?" said Cor, moving with the fox, trying not to pull at the hair. Weh stepped a little, saying, "That's not so bad." And mover faster to curl around a bush, slapping the leaves into Cors' face. Everyone laughed and Weh apologized.

"You have to think about that when you move through the forest- although I've seen Ryk do it to Pip often just for fun." Said Roo and added: "Fen, you lead the way, you've discovered much of the area already."

Fen moved up the hill past the deep crevasse. It was a gradual slope but always upwards. He warned about and veered away from deep fissures in the stony surface, pointing out the place where he slept and the animals who lived here and there.

Pip had taken the newcomers with him along the river towards Ryk's tree. Mac, Kam and Blu were all eyes and gaping mouths at the wonderous fast river, its high bank cut here and there with tiny falls running down from the forested hills above. Clear as air, the wide river flowed over the time-worn smooth rocks near the shore. Looking further from the bank, the stones visibility faded into darkness that told of depth at the rivers centre. The day was fine, clear, and sunny; here at the bank a fine cooling breeze made small wavelets on the surface.

"I wonder what it's like on the other side of the river." Blu watched a hawk dip into the water and carry a fish away to the trees on the other side.

"It seemed the same as here when Dub took us through, but I didn't get a great chance to look around, we were high up and moving fast. There is a nice aspen grove and the river seemed quieter above the falls."

Another raccoon was with Ryk, one Pip had never met.

"This is Ine, she has just arrived here from up the hill. She is looking for a new home-place."

Pip wiggled his eyebrow at Ryk then turned to the small female, "We are new here also, but this is a good place, now that the wolverine is gone."

Ryk winked at Pip and led the young raccoon to where unsuspecting fish were milling in a pool.

Lis and Tym showed Lyl and her father around, first to the lily shelter there and then to look at the smelly carcass. They wandered mostly easterly, parallel to the river. Hep marvelled at the abundance of rodents, in comparison to the environment around Home Tree where it needed time to recuperate from the heavy hunting from owls and foxes. Sudden movement through the trees- it was Tich doing his best to reduce the population. The forest was different from home, always on a slope, with mostly coniferous trees. It had the green piney scent, full of cool shadows, russet needles caught between mossy boulders. The trees were alive with squirrels and birds, at this moment making a tumult of tweets, caws, chitters and squeaks.

Moving the leaning stones from the salt vein for Hep to inspect it, Tym saw movement just above the hole. It was a chipmunk hopping in a fast scurry towards them, "Help! Help!" It turned and ran back the way it had come, over rocks, roots and around fern clumps. They hurried after the waving tail, curious. Hearing plaintive squeaks from ahead they brushed through a spriggy crowfoot plant to see the biggest spider web any of them had ever seen. It stretched across two large pines and at the lower side of it was a struggling chipmunk, caught tight to the sticky net. At the top of the net was the desiccated body of a small bird, and between this and the new victim was a very large fat spider. The Crum were unfamiliar with this giant breed, with its legs stretched out it was almost has wide as a bird with a round abdomen the size of an acorn nut. Hep reached the chipmunk first. He had taken a stone knife from his hunting pouch and prepared to cut away the web when the spider shot a web at his hand. The spider moved and his hand was stuck onto the web along with the frightened wide-eyed chipmunk. Although the Crum yelled and threatened, the spider couldn't understand them and didn't care, it had never seen the likes of these green topped grey creatures, maybe they tasted good.

It would take a group effort. Hep told Lis and Lyl to climb either pine to cut away the anchoring strands. Tym used his spear to hold the large spider at bay, stabbing at it as it came close to the chipmunk and the caught Crum. When it realized the vibrations in its web was the loosening of its structure it scampered up to Liz who saw it coming and ducked a shooting web from its spinneret. She and Lyl cut and sliced and avoided the web shots while Tym cleared a furious Hep from the trap. They both then worked at releasing the chipmunk. The whole web suddenly dropped next to them with an angry spider jumping on top of the chipmunk. Just before its fangs could descend the combined spears of Tym and Hep cut it into two.

"That was close. I don't think it could have got through our skin but I'm glad it didn't get a chance to try. "Hep shuddered. The chipmunks had left after many bobbing thanks. "This is a story to tell the clan, they will never believe it." Lyl kicked at the corpse with its curled in legs.

Cor and Roo had got down from the foxes to drink from a small pool surrounded by wavey ferns and star shaped flowers. It had been a steep climb in places and the foxes needed a break, the riders would hike on their own for a while. Roo was met by a group of grey squirrels, bushy tails quivering. He told them about the Crum and how he wanted to meet the animals here. Squirrels, like the rabbits, had simple thoughts. Roo and Cor heard: "Good- good- good. We happy. Busy-busy!" before the fast scrabble up the trunk.

This far away from the wolverines hunting ground the animals were plentiful and healthy.

They met a small clutch of hares who expressed thankfulness that the wolverine and wolf were gone. Their den was in one of the clefts in the stone where they had dug into a vein of soft earth. They disappeared into the seemingly bottomless hole, white flags of rear tails flipping.

Ascending the hill until they came to a vertical wall, they turned around to just breath, enjoying the view of evergreen tops flowing like a blanket to the silver flash of the river. As Roo turned to go, he saw a dark place along the cliff. "Was it another cave?" he asked himself. They carefully moved over loose gravel to the cave, for that was what it was. It had a crude wood door canted open, the entrance a little shorter than Cor.

There was a familiar glow coming from inside! They recognized the warm light given off the phosphorescent mushrooms. Slowly they went in, Roo ducking in the narrow doorway. The 'shrooms were in a several simple vats full of moist moss in just the same way they had to light the cave back at Home Tree. Who did this? There was an empty nest bed and stone tools. Their gaze was suddenly caught by the amazingly painted walls. It was a Crum story, just like the historical carvings in the Home Tree burrow. It showed many Crum leaving a much younger Home Tree, the travels, dangers, adventures and what could only be mountains. There was a home burrow under a tree with a backdrop of a mountain, near a lake. Then a disaster, the burrow tree hit by lightning, many Crum dead. Roo was astonished, but when he turned to his mother, she looked shocked but also something else, a sad look of knowing.

A sound from the entrance, a crunch on the gravel outside and they turned- a strange Crum was silhouetted, blocking some of the sunlight.

His voice was hoarse, unused to speaking. "I am found." He croaked.

He was a Crum, but without a shum, dressed in rough furs. He carried a good stone tipped spear and a full looking sturdy hunting pouch. Dirty Green hair shot with white told his age at over middle years, dark brown eyes that had witnessed years of pain. When Roo thought, "who are you?", he answered: "I am Dre, last of the mountain clan."

Cor thought, "Oh no!" and Dre looked at her.

"I see you know of us."

To Roos surprise she nodded. He blurted, "What is this?!"

Dre said, "Come out in the sunlight, there is a place I like to sit at."

He led them to a small clearing with a low shelf of rock at perfect sitting height, overlooking the forest. Roo and Cor sat while Dre faced them. Roo asked, "Mema, what do you know of this clan?"

Without answering him she turned to Dre, "What do you mean you are the last?"

"I've painted my history just in case I never found the old Home Tree that I was told about. It's been a hard journey; I didn't know where to look for it."

"How come I've never heard of your clan?" asked Roo to them both.

Cor patted Roo's hand and sighed. "Because only the leaders pass down the story. It is our great shame, a history that we cover up, a decision that was made hundreds of years ago and not one I would probably have made."

Dre interjected angrily, "We were too different! They feared us!"

"I'm not sure that was it, but to be able to hear other Crum thoughts and not the animals made your ancestors impossible to live with. That's what I was told."

Roo was shocked, both at the angry face and his mother's justification.

Dre: "It started with my great, great, great grandmother; she was born with mind-reading of Crum instead of animals. She hid it, told no one until she had a partner, and her offspring were the same way. Then it wasn't a secret anymore and the other Crum found it hard to be around them. But they couldn't hear each other, just the 'normal' Crum. It was unsettling for the clan to have their most private thoughts heard; plus, they couldn't live in harmony with the animals.

Roo was thinking: "We are co-dwellers with our animals, they help us in our gathering, hunting, and warning of dangers, that must have been very difficult."

Dre nodded, "We finally had to leave, there were twenty-five of us then. There were two Crum like you with us, animal talkers, and they had two rabbits to carry most of our essentials. We founded a good burrow up in the mountains." At this he indicated over the high cliff. "There is a small valley up there. In time the two Crum who could talk to the rabbits passed on and the rabbits and their descendants returned to the wild. We were okay, though, a small group. We couldn't hear each other's thoughts and forgot about it once the two had died. A few generations passed; it was hard without being able use the help of animals, but we managed. We wore furs from the small animals that we could kill. I think you call that a shum?" Dre pointed at the cowl-cape around Roo's neck. We had no way to make them, no shum trees. Our population was kept low from predator attacks and a lack of knowledge of the medicinal plants."

"I was very young, about forty, when the storm hit. I was hunting and was waiting out the rain in another shelter and luckily my parents were in a leather curing workshop when lightning hit the Home Tree. It was terrible! Everyone in the burrow died, burned, or killed. My parents were thrown from the workshop but only stunned."

Roo watched the tears stream down the grey face, filling the sharp creases made from such a hard life.

"We made a small home out of the hunting shelter, but it was hard just the three of us. Before they died, they told me about the Home Tree that our clan had been expelled from but the knowledge of where it was had been lost. I've been looking, every few years I moved. This year I was going to travel again. I've been seven seasons in this cave."

They were all quiet. Dre couldn't help but be aware of their thinking. Roo: "He must come home with us." At the same time from Cor: "He can't stay with us, it's so sad. I'm still the leader of our clan. We will have to vote on this, this could divide us."

Dre answered the unspoken opinions, "I'm sorry, yes, I could meet the others, but I can't stay with you."

Cor lowered her eyes in embarrassment and Roo was shaken to realize a-new that his ruminations were plain to Dre.

"I've started a new burrow here, by the water where the wolverine lived, will you meet all of us?"

"Is that mean critter gone? That's good. I could never go near there. He would have bit me in two for the fun of it." Dre finally smiled. It was a sweet smile that changed his whole face, making him look younger.

"If you know where he had lived, that's our new burrow. Allow us time to tell everyone, there are thirteen of us, then could you come to a feast tomorrow?"

Dre said yes, he would come to the evening meal.

Cor and Roo found the foxes at the pool. They climbed on top of them saying, "Hurry back to the burrow, okay?" As Fen turned to go, he saw the other Crum waving. Surprised, Fen asked, "Who's that?"

"I'll tell you as we go." And he did, while the two foxes carefully went downhill, sometimes leaping from stone to lower stone, making the Crum hold tight to neck and mane.

As soon as the evening meal concluded and everyone finished talking about the sites and the spider, Cor stood and told them about Dre. To say they were shocked was to put it mildly.

"How could they just throw out Crum that way?" Cin was visibly upset.

Bry, who had stayed behind to keep watch for the day, asked Cor curtly, "Why did the leaders keep this from us?

"This secret has been kept for almost six hundred years. I might not have agreed with it but after all this time it became a tradition kept for all the leaders. They had no longer charted their route; no animal must have reported where they were. I'm sorry, it's terrible what has happened, but he can't stay with us.

Kam asked, "Why ever not? He's alone!" Cor said nothing to this, but Roo gave an answer, "I think you will see when you meet him, it's a little unsettling to have your thoughts plain to him."

Cor looked at all the Crum in turn, "I won't make this decision alone; we will have a good feast for him tomorrow."

They could see Dre coming, He had cleaned up for them, but Cra could see the worn fur patches and the rends in his boots. The foxes, bobcat and raccoons all stayed up in the trees, not wanting to make the new Crum nervous.

The group, in a clump circled Dre to welcome him. It was Cra who realized his distress as he backed away and held his head. "The clamour!" he cried.

"Stop! Everyone back away." She ordered. "It's too much for him."

Cra walked up to him by herself, saying kindly, "I'm sorry. It must be hard to have all our noise in your head at once. How about we come to you one at a time?"

Dre, grateful, gave her a shaky smile.

So, in singles, they met Dre and then moved away. They bought him food then went back to the sitting stones, allowing him to come closer at his leisure. Eventually he came to within seven feet and stood, "From here I can't hear all of you and I can be easy, you see I've never experienced this- The elders would talk of it- this is what you have with your animals."

"And there is some of us that do very little thinking." Cra looked at her brother, laughing.

"Hey!" Pip pretended to be offended.

Cin gave Dre a new shum, his first ever, and showed him how it was worn.

Mac, seeing that Dre had the same size feet, gave him his new pair of rat leather boots. Hep gladly handed over new shirts and pants saying he'd make new ones when he got home.

Brown eyes glistening and overcome with all the heartfelt generosity, Dre said thank you for everything and that he needed to be alone now.

Roo led him to the lily shelter where he could spend the night. They had set up a nice nest bed and laid out food secured in a closed basket. Fen kept watch from a nearby spruce. He wouldn't go close until Dre became used to him.

When Roo returned, the Crum sat around discussing the revelations.

"I should have anticipated that we would be too much for him, even without the mind reading, he'd find so many of us difficult after being alone for so long." Cor said.

"I'm thinking that it should be Dre's decision to be with us and how much. It might take time to adjust, and only he knows how much is too much- we are a noisy lot." Stated Cra.

From Lyl: "There must be a way to have both, to allow him to be part of our community without distressing him.

Tym spoke, a little cautious, "Is anyone else finding it a little creepy that he'd always know what we are thinking?" This earned him a few nods of agreement.

"Yah, I could be thinking of my sweet Kam!" Mac wiggled his eyebrow at his partner who blushed and laughed softly.

Cor didn't say it out loud but worried about what they should say to the Home Tree clan, or even if they should.

The morning sun was softened by a fog over the river that coated it and crept up the bank to the new burrow. Before it cleared, Roo who was the first up, found Dre with his feet dangling over the grassy edge where there was room for only two Crum to sit at a time- something that Roo thought he did on purpose. He was wearing his new clothes, the warm shum lightly covering his head. Roo handed him a leaf of fresh fish and blueberries. He ate hungrily. Roo sat and let his thoughts drift over the sun sparkling water.

"It's easier with male Crum, you know. "Dre smiled at Roo, and continued the thought:

"Us males have purpose driven thinking and sometimes 'no thinking' moments. Females seem to be always thinking, it never stops." Roo laughed with him.

"It's your choice, I think you could stay close to us, but you might find it hard to live in our burrow." Sober-faced, Roo watched for Dre's reaction.

"Your Cra is kind, and I like you and Pip very much; but you are right, I can't stay in your burrow, it would be too loud in that space; but I'm a good hunter, I can help."

"We have been mostly using our animals to do the killing, it's hard for us to hear the cries of the small animals. Fen must eat anyway, so he lets me skin the bodies before he cleans up the mess. My mema was a hunter when she was young and wants to hunt again on Weh and stop being the clan leader."

"Yes, I got some of that from her when we met." Pausing, he added, "Tell her don't worry, I don't want to go to the Home Tree anymore, but I'd like to have my story told."

Roo thought, "Just how old are you?" and Dre answered with a smile, "I am one-hundred and fifty-four I think, my many seasons have passed without notice."

CHAPTER NINE

FINDING A NEW NORMAL

Tich and Weh obediently laid flat, tummy's to the dirt as the half-filled baskets were placed on them. Fen bumped snouts with his daughter, saying be careful and say hello to the family. Tich felt like an adult compared to Weh and tried to act as mature as he could, barely allowing the Crum to scratch behind his ears. Dre stood above on the hill watching the leave-taking, the Crum had one at a time said their goodbyes. When Lyl had approached him, he said, "Good luck at South Burrow, be happy." Lyl glowed and thanked him, knowing that no one had told him, he had heard it from herself.

Cor held his hands, saying nothing out loud, thought, "I wish you happiness, I will tell them, don't worry."

Hep surprised him with a hug, saying "Look after them."

Cin and Bry said they were coming back in the spring. "I'll bring Tools." Said Bry.

"I'll bring strawberries!" Cin told him.

The North Burrow fell into a routine, one watcher on the hemlock branch above the burrow always. Dre stayed in the lily shelter after they made it more permanent with a supporting roof of wood under the lichen patch and bracing plank walls to carry the weight. This allowed for a good door. Dre had returned to his cave to retrieve his things but was very happy with the arrangement, especially as they shared a larger variety of delicious food with him. Roo's group allowed Dre to pick how much interaction he had with them, happy to have him for meals or visits but sometimes he disappeared for days. When he did this, he would leave an ochre-coloured stone leaning against his door to indicate that he was out exploring. Both Fen and Ryk started digging their own dens in preparation for winter, Ryks, of course, nearer the water.

A one-bed Make-well was made in a nook at the back of the burrow near the small exit there. Cra filled shelves and baskets with everything she thought they might need.

Kam and Mac completed the pantry that Cin had started, fashioning vats and containers for the communal food stuffs. Everyone helped to fill them daily although Kam took on the responsibility of organizing and cleaning it daily.

They needed a controlled water flow to go through the burrow and Pip, Blu and Lis worked on rerouting some of the waterfall water to be channelled into stone pipes. They also worked on further redirection of rain run-off from large downpours (as demonstrated one wickedly rainy day.) That day the pretty little waterfall had become a gushing torrent, almost washing away the seating stones.

It was Roo's job to meet with all the animals on the hillside and ask them to report on any new intruders or problems. He told them of Cra and the Make-Well, to come there if they had any small hurts. Besides the many birds, squirrels, chipmunks, rats, mice, voles, moles and a drove of hare; Roo found a family of shoats by the river, small snakes and frogs galore. Passing through were herds deer and some black fox. Dub found a beehive in a large hollow tree, thankfully not too close to the burrow, and Cra asked Dub to only get at a little of the waxy honey, not to destroy the whole nest so everyone could enjoy the sweet gift.

Dub visited frequently; the first time had Dre fleeing towards his old cave until Roo could tell him that the bear was a friend. The large bears visits had the benefit of his marking this as part of his territory. Any wolves, cougars or other predators would scent his 'pee' notices and avoid the Crum's hillside.

Two owls lived on either side of what Roo marked as Crum land, a spotted owl, close to the great falls and a hawk owl who had a nest near Dre's cave. The hawk owl wanted nothing to do with Crum, but the spotted owl was friendly, stopping to tell Roo about his life when Roo had evening watches.

One night while Roo watched the moon glow over the river, Coy, the spotted owl told him about the large nest being built across the water on top of very tall pine. "Eagles or hawks maybe, big anyway. "Said the owl. "I'd like to avoid them if I could!" Roo, who once had a terrifying experience with an eagle, agreed with the small owl.

In the morning light he could see the nest where a white head popped up and then a large brown bird joined it carrying more branches.

The eagle soared silently on the thermals over the river, watching for the undulating movement of fish that he could snatch up for a meal to take to his mate. The eagles kept away from the more active shore, the strange grey creatures that had come had brought foxes, raccoons, and a bobcat.

The air was cooler today, autumn a suggestion in the slight yellowing of the treetops. Just has the eagle was about to give up he saw a flash of sun on scales near one of the grey creatures. Sweeping down in the wind, he stretched out one talon to spear through the surface fish and the other snagged at the grey creature's wrapping (Skin? Fur?) he thought. One large downstroke of the wings took the eagle high over the river. The squirming of its prey was normal but when the creature wiggled and yelled in his head to put him down, he was surprised into opening his grip enough that the weird prey was dropped from the great height into the river.

Dre was the only witness to Pip's danger. He threw aside his spear and hunting pouch and dove into the river, spearing cleanly to where Pip was last seen. Coming to the surface he could see Pip flaying and bobbing, being pulled down the eastward current. Dre swam with all his strength to catch up with him.

Ryk was moving along the shore and saw the action as it passed him. He pursued the two Crum from the land, crashing through the thick brush. Pip went down again, no longer moving his arms, just as Dre reached him. He grabbed at Pip's shum, pulling, then wrapped his arm around Pips neck and shoulder while kicking fiercely to stay afloat. He slowly angled towards the shore. The river widened, the current less fast, and Dre finally found foot-purchase. He dragged Pip ashore. He wasn't breathing. Sitting with Pip propped, bent in front him, Dre squeezed, hugging Pip hard and forcing a fountain of river out of Pip with each thrust. Then Dre laid Pip on his back and smashed his fist onto Pips chest, once, twice, three times. Pip gasped and breathed but stayed unconscious. Ryk arrived, panting, with a torn and bleeding ear and twigs stuck in his fur. Dre said to him: "We have to get him back!" But all Ryk heard was the Crum sounds of deep chirps. Fortunately, he didn't need to understand to know what was needed. Ryk lowered his shoulder next to Pip and Dre maneuverer Pip on to him, climbing on in back to hold Pip with one arm, the other clamped into the heavy neck fur. Moving fast but carefully, they brought Pip to the burrow. They were spotted before getting near, the Crum running alongside Ryk. Roo and Blu carried Pip into the Make-well nook where Cra, with Roo's help undressed her brother and covered him in warm furs. Dre had disappeared outside while she and Roo had worked over Pip, Cra looking him over and listening to his chest. "I think he's going to be, fine, though I must admit I'm unsure of myself over how he has survived. My teachings on Crum drownings are sadly pessimistic."

Roo stepped out of the entrance to sit by Dre who had waited to see if Pip would be okay. "He's sleeping and we hope to see him wake up soon. He had some bruising on his chest but no other injuries."

Dre smiled at this, "Yeah, I had to push the water out of him and start his heart again." Roo, taken aback, blurted, "You did what?!"

"We were living by a lake, remember? All my clan had to learn to save each other. I think you have not been in much deep water."

"I was but I don't remember it." Roo told him the tale of his getting swept away after hitting his head. Dre smiled a little at Roo's memory of the river otter dragging him out of the water, thinking he might be good to eat.

"Thank you, and Ryk says thank you, too." The raccoon was loitering near them. Ryk said to Roo, "He was amazing! He swam like a fish!"

"Dre, could you teach us this? I think we are going to need this here. This might not be the last time someone falls in the river."

The soft light from a large niche of mushroom painted the scene in the Make-Well alcove with gold and ochres, Cra and Mar hovered over the fur mound of Pip in the one nest bed. Pip woke with a groan, holding his sore chest and coughing a barking watery cough. "Oohh.... What happened? The eagle...I was in the river!"

"Dre saved you." Cra told him. She had kept watch with Roo for many hours. Tears stood in her copper eyes, so like his.

"I have to thank him, but how did he do it?"

"He's going to teach us. He grew up by a lake and all his clan could swim."

Moving slowly, Pip climbed up to the Lily shelter where Dre sat enjoying the waving ivory blooms.

"How are you feeling?" asked Dre politely. Pip moved carefully to sit beside him, holding his arms across his torso while emitting a few deep croaking coughs.

"I hope someday I can return the favour and smack you around." joked Pip. Turning serious he finished with a heartfelt, "Thank you. I've spent all my life in the creek, but this river is deep and fast. You can swim! I want to be your first student."

CHAPTER TEN

GOING DOWNRIVER

Pip watched the large log float past him. It was easily as wide as Ryk and ten times as long. It hardly rolled or turned, at least half of the wood staying dry above the water. He asked himself, "What if I were on that log and where is it going? I need to talk to Dre."

He adjusted his spear across his back and closed his hunting pouch that lay against his hip.

It was a clear and sunny afternoon, and he was finished with his morning fishing and didn't have a watch duty for two days. Idle and restless and suddenly excited with this new idea, Pip climbed the bank and entered the forest in search of Dre.

The North group all knew how to swim now though some took better to the water than others. Pip was the best of the bunch, He never wanted to feel that helpless in the river again. Bry and Tym were the worst swimmers, like cats not wanting to get their feet wet, but they suffered through it. Everyone was taught the life saving techniques. Dre used Pip as his model, Pip hamming it up as the distressed and abused drowning Crum that had everyone laughing. They did their training in the shallower water where Pip had been rescued, the river widened there, and it had a slow drop off before becoming deeper. The water was warmer there too, a good thing as the Crum all had to strip down out their leather and suede clothing.

Pip found Dre helping Kam to carry a large basket of fern and dandelion leaves into the burrow. The pantry was just inside the door, a small room that was filled with shelves laden with bowls and vats with baskets on the floor and a water trough passing though on one side. It smelled amazing to Dre, earthy mushrooms, fragrant flowers, spicey herbs and meaty grubs. He let down the basket and snuck a grub, grinning and hearing Kams' laughing thanks in his head as he departed out the open door.

"Can I ask you something? Pip motioned to the seating stones. Dre munched and waited for Pip's question.

"Two things, I guess: What is past our swimming place further down river and, on your lake, did you ever make something that floated, that you could stand or sit on?"

"I'll answer the second thing first, yes, we made boats." Pips mind was clear to Dre, he saw the floating log, and Pip thinking: Wow! A boat?

He laughed, "We carved them from dry logs and pushed them with poles and paddles. Only when the weather was good and the water smooth. It was one way to cross the lake but not very fast, so we used them mostly for fun. I can show you how we made them but if you went on this river I would caution you, you don't know where you'll end up and how to get back here. I've explored only as far as the gorge and had to stop there. The gorge is wild and deep, impossible to cross.

Pip nodded, "It's something I must think about. What do you know of this area around us?"

"I've told Roo this, it's part of my story but I'm happy to tell you too. After I buried my parents under the trees, I went in search of the Home Tree that I was told about. We called our lake the Great Bear Lake and the mountain that was always reflected there, the Great Bear Mountain. It's beautiful, but I was very lonely. I went south the first summer, but the land was uphill and moving towards more mountains, so I turned back and tried west. That way I think if I had continued, I might have eventually found the Home Tree, but I was bitten by a large snake and almost died. It wasn't poisonous but its fang went right through my thigh. I killed the snake to get myself loose and I bled a lot. Afterwards it was hard to walk. I returned to Great Bear to recover over the winter and woke up better but very weak. A large wolf pack had moved into the valley, and I was afraid to stay there so I left again I came over the valleys hills towards here. I found the river but with the wolverine, I stayed away from his territory. Then I found my cave and it was home for a while. That's where Roo and Cor found me. So, to answer your question, no, I don't know where the river goes. I never made it east and I've only walked a short way past your swimming place."

Pip stared at the quiet river surface, today a deep marine blue. "I must think about it. I think I'll ask if anyone wants to explore along the shore towards the east, at least for a few days before making a boat. But I have to say, I'd really love to make a boat!"

"I will come with you and when you are ready, I'll help you with the boat. Has for going on the boat ride, that will be too much adventure for my old body."

That evening Pip asked the group who would like to go east with him and Dre along the river.

Roo looked at Cra who answered the unspoken question with, "Not too long, Okay?"

Lis and Tym wanted to join them. Roo said, "That's all I think, we can't have too many gone from here at once. What about animals? Are we walking or riding?"

It was Pip who answered this, "Walking. What if they are attacked? Let's leave them here to guard the Burrow."

They travelled in single file, the bush thick and close along this span. Where there was a wide enough beach, they went along by the water and where they couldn't, they climbed into the forest. The last two days revealed nothing remarkable, the land and water much the same as the place they came from. The nights they spent up large trees, finding crooks in the fattest branches.

Most of the time, Pip went ahead, then Roo, Lis and Tym with Dre at the rear. As the oldest he was the slowest, sometime finding his old wound bothering him if the climbing was very strenuous. The river gradually curved north, and the composition of the trees changed from the tall straight red and white pines to stunted black spruce, scrub pines and yellowing tamarack struggling to grow around giant glacier deposits. They found themselves having to climb sheer rock faces, sometimes easier to stay up in the close packed trees and cross over touching branches. On the end of the third day the struggling five were on the surface again, finally cresting the steepest hill yet. They could go no further. A deep gorge with a wild river was emptying into their river far below the barren ridge where they stood panting. They watched the water rush and foam around huge stones at the junction that had broken off from the rough cracked walls of the gorge.

Across the way the land sloped down again, they could see far away, the turn of the river moving east, to a gentling forest that was brightened with large leafed deciduous trees.

"That's where we need to get to!" said Pip as he wiped his face with his shum.

"It looks just like our forest at Home Tree." Lis squatted down to drop off her backpack, open it and pass out juicy berries. They hadn't found a place to drink water since starting up this hill and their water bottles were empty.

"We need to go back down, we need water." Tym thanked her and ate the blueberry, careful not to lose any of the juice.

Roo said: "I wonder if there is a way across farther up the gorge."

Dre sat down the massage his aching thigh and looked in the direction of the source of the new river. It was straight and deep, finally disappearing in a far curve.

A voice came into the heads of Pip, Roo, Lis and Tym: "Yes, I'd like to get across there too, but I've never found a way."

Startled, they turned and had to look up, way up at a mountain lion standing just behind them. Dre looked around to see what had made them jump and had to clutch at his heart, scared to move or speak.

It took a second of just looking at each other before Roo concluded that the lion meant no threat to them, so he said, "Hello. I'm Roo. We are Crum."

"Oh, I know about the Crum. I've been aware of your passage through my forest."

"How is it you know about us?" Pip asked. Instead of answering Pip, he said:

"What's wrong with him?" The lion moved his great head to indicate Dre who was carefully backing away, scooting on bum, heels, and palms.

"This is Dre. He can't hear you or any animal, he hears us instead. You are making him nervous."

Dre said to the other Crum, "I hear your side of the conversation. It's just that a mountain lion killed one of my clan members long ago, so we have always been afraid of them." Roo repeated this to the lion.

"Ah, I see. That was how I know of you. It is part of the knowledge that has been passed down from mother to cub, not to try to eat a Crum because the taste is very bad. As for understanding what you are saying, that's new to me but I've been hearing you since you passed by my hiding place two days ago." The lion backed away from them along the precipice of the gorge and gracefully laid down, curling in his great paws and swirling his long tail in front of his dusk-coloured body. "Tell him to relax, I won't bite." At this he grinned, showing enormous fangs and sharp teeth made for rending.

Roo gave him a crooked half smile, "That's not helping!" and laughed.

"I know, I couldn't help myself. I am called Lon, son of Firi."

Roo introduced each Crum who bowed at their spoken names. Dre had stood by now and bowed also, finally releasing a sigh, and venturing a smile.

Lon led them down the hill and further into the forest to a large pond surrounded by moss-coated boulders and thick pine trunks. There they filled their water bottles and quenched their thirst. Lis took a tool from her pack and dug out water snails and grubs from around the pool. After a quick swish in the water, she tossed each Crum the fresh food as they sat around talking with the lion. When she threw a large one at Lon, he snapped it out of the air in a neat bite.

Lon told them that he covered great areas in his travels, he knew about the wolves at Great Bear valley and where the wolverine lived and even knew about Dub though they had never met.

Roo explained to Lon his purpose in meeting all the animals he could so that he could teach all the Crum about their traits and dangers.

"We are all dangerous to something, even you carry a spear and eat tiny creatures." Said the languid feline.

It had been a difficult day, the light fading fast in the already dim forest. After witnessing several yawns, Lon bid them to come spend the night in his den, a small cave in the rock outcropping.

They woke to an empty den. At the pond Lon had clawed fresh furrows in the mud to expose a milling group of beetles that had yet to escape into the soil. The group didn't wait to see the lion but started out on the return to the river on the path to home. They thought if he wanted to see them, he could easily catch up to the small Crum. They were almost at the place along the river where the steep bank had forced them into the forest when Lon appeared. The big cat had moved silently from shadow to shadow until stepping finally into the light right in front of the Crum.

"I wanted to say good luck and goodbye. If you ever find a way to get to the other side, past the rapids, I'd like to know." Lon nodded and blinked round orbs of yellow shot with green. The Crum all bowed to the cat and said thank you for the beetles and thank you for letting us stay with you. With that the lion disappeared into the shadows again.

Pip couldn't let it go, he wanted to make a boat, to find that other forest past the gorge. He didn't know how he could come back yet and worried a little that he might never get back. The summer was getting along, the autumn cooling temps had begun to paint the highest treetops with warmer tones of olives and grey.

It seemed like a wish granted when one morning he found a large, drifted log moored on the shallow beach where they had been swimming. After it dried out for several days, he carolled Ryk and Fen into strapping themselves on to it and hauling it higher up the bank. Dre walked around it, inspecting the grain and the jutting broken limbs all around it.

It became a group project with everyone but Cra helping to saw, cut, shave and scrape a boat-like shape out of it. Its final size was as wide as a fat raccoon and three times as long. It wasn't quite done when winter descended and put a halt to the project. With the animals help they turned the boat over, now much lighter, and painted the bottom with pine sap. They would get it finished in the spring.

CHAPTER ELEVEN

GOING EAST

Roo opened his eyes to the dim light of the mushrooms and the sound of rain gurgling through and around the burrow. He realized the air above the furs covering him was warmer, it must be spring, and he was starving. Next to him curled his sweet Cra, just starting to slit open her pretty eyes.

On the other side of the wall, Pips eyes popped open, his first thought was hunger, and then, how was his boat? He pulled on his leather clothes and boots and hurried out the door.

Dre had a nest bed nearest the entrance and had already dressed and left the burrow after pushing away the doors securing stones and grabbing digging tools and a basket on the way out. Everyone would be hungry, and he had no wish to hear the groups waking thoughts.

Blu heard the rain and listened for leaks. He was skilled enough to hear that sure enough, there was some repair work needed; but it could wait till he filled his growling stomach.

Mac and Kam snuggled closer, wanting to keep out the rest of the world for a little longer and be together.

Lis awoke and began to uncurl her stout frame, pushing away the furs from her face. She was never fast at coming out of her torpor whether it was the hibernation-spring-wake-up or the dawn awareness of a new day begun. She was hungry. Pip had his boat almost finished. Who would take that dangerous trip with him? Should she go? It was that thought that woke her up fully.

Tym pushed off the covering furs feeling too hot, stretched out stiff legs to hang outside of the nest bed. He needed food and lots of it. Sitting on the edge of the round bed he pushed fingers through his light green spiky hair and thought of his brother and parents at Home Tree. Before he fell into his winter sleep he had decided to go with Pip on his boat.

By the time Cra left the burrow it had stopped raining. All surfaces were wet and shining, the sun breaking through the loosening cloud cover. She had always found he first view of the outdoor changes in the spring fascinating and invigorating. The sound hit her first, the plop-plopping of drips was overlayed with bird song, countless chatters and calls greeting the morning. A lot of branches both big and small had fallen and needed to be moved or used, a new layer of dropped leaves littered the ground but pushing through it, the bright new sprigs of growth. Evergreen trees held the needle filled boughs over the year, now they were tipped with bright clumps of new tight furls of leaves. The river was high, well up on the bank, showing none of its former landing stones.

Roo and Dre were coming through the trees with a food-filled basket between them, each free hand not holding the handles was stuffing food into their mouths. Fen was following, shaking winter fluffy fur. He didn't hibernate and had spent a comfortable winter hunting when not sleeping in his new den. Behind Fen was a stranger, a young shy fox who hesitated before the burrow landing.

She walked closer to the two fox to meet and welcome them "This is Mai, she joined me in my den over the winter."

"Hello Mai, I'm so glad to meet you. I am a healer here, come to me if you need any help." She was pretty and small with lighter coloured fur than Fens.

"We will be having a litter of pups this summer, my first. Fen will let you know when it's time if I need any help. Thank you." Cra looked at Fen who was smiling his toothy grin. She was surprised to see he had a lot of white on his muzzle fur now.

After they had left, she sat with all the burrow Crum at the seating stones and ate the first spring meal, freshly sprouted shoots of fern and creamy grubs. When their basic hunger had been satisfied, they could get more sophisticated in the menu but for now, simple and nourishing was best.

Pip told them of his morning's discovery: "Ryk has a new litter, four kits, a pair of each type. Ine is still nursing but they are keeping them both busy. They keep escaping and getting into trouble."

Roo asked the question they were all thinking, "How is your boat?"

Dre, who was sitting apart on a stone he had designated as his, told them, "We haven't turned it over yet and a family of ground squirrels had made a winter nest under it, but I scooted them out, I hope they didn't mind but I think they might have scolded me a little."

Pip laughed and added, "I came upon the scene with Dre holding up his hands, surrounded by quivering annoyed squirrels calling him "Flea-scum and maggot head." "Squirrels have great insults!"

Dre shrugged, "Good thing I didn't know what they were saying. If Ryk and Fen can be spared, the boat needs to be turned over. I didn't see any of the cracking in the wood grain that I was worried about."

Cra repeated what she had spoken about when this boat was being made, "Doesn't any of you think this is a terrible idea? Pip and anyone that goes with him will be as helpless as a leaf on the river surface, where will they end up and how will they get back?"

Pip was firm with his sister, "You know I must go, it's all I've been thinking about. We won't be coming back from this side of the river for sure, the gorge will stop us. It will have to be from across the river on the other side, unless we find another bear to carry us to this side, I will travel the route that Dub took, the slow climb to the escarpment."

Roo understood both sides and wanted to keep the peace. He told them, "They won't be going for a while, there is much work to be done. In the meantime, we have jobs to do around here, watches to begin again now that we are awake, food to gather and store, bedding to clean out and replace, the burrow smells like a bear cave and Blu tells me we have a leak to fix."

Dre added, "I need to fix my roof at the lily shelter and air out everything. Thank you for allowing me to stay with you over the season".

Acky dropped down in the clearing. "It's about time you woke up! I have heard through the other crows that you will have company coming from your Home Tree soon, they said to expect them in two weeks, after the twins finish the shum harvest."

Roo thanked the crow who flew away with a gift of a tossed grub. They had much to do.

It was a wet a bedraggled collection of travellers that arrived from the southwest, Tich leading with the twins on his back and two large baskets strapped on. The Bobcat had reached his adult size in height and filled out in musculature. He was now almost twice the size of Fen though far behind in maturity. Following Tich strode an adult and stronger Weh, carrying Bry and Cin with baskets of the promised strawberry plants and tools along with walnuts and charcoal, birch paper, bottles various juices. Walking behind the animals were Cor, Til and the big surprise: Jmy from South burrow.

Roo yelled and threw himself at his older brother in an enormous back-slapping hug. Cor joined in, she had missed Roo and loved seeing her sons together again. The twins hugged everyone, they had grown and if it was possible, even more beautiful. Bry and Cin went to the lily shelter to find Dre who had stayed away from the large gathering. After the gift giving, (Dre had wild garlic bulbs for Cin and a new spear for Bry,) He told them that he would meet to newcomers in the morning, one at a time.

"Jmy, how is Myn? How is South Burrow and how is Lyl doing? Roo asked his brother. They were at the welcome feast, the seating stones augmented with to with a large, chopped branch. Cor and Cra listened beside them, shoulders touching, comforted by being in each other's company again.

"Myn is good, very busy with learning shum making with Bip, Ryh and Mir. (Cra and Pips mother who Cor told her was doing fine, sends her hugs) South burrow has grown with ten new younglings. They keep everyone active and running. Lyl is very happy with Gyn, she is making a new leather curing shop with his help. Myn and I walked from there to Home Tree, I was concerned about riding on Phax when I heard about Tich living in the Home Tree area. Two males, a bobcat and a lynx might not get along. I wanted to see this new burrow. Mema tells me that you only have one watcher at a time in your tree?" Jmy waved his hand at Blu, up on the hemlock branch, keeping an eye on the party as well as the forest.

"I'm working with the animals to be my warning helpers. We have no large snakes here and our big advantage is Dub, our bear friend who comes by often. Let me tell you about Lon..."

Pip sat with the two brothers, Lis and the twins. The talk was all about the boat.

"We left part of a branch on the logs bottom to act as a keel. That's what Dre says we need to make it stay upright. We could go out to it in the morning, it needs paddles and more sap painted on the bottom. I think we could be ready to go soon..."

Bry and Cin were happy to be back at the North Burrow, they had missed the quiet ruggedness as well as the Crum. While Kam and Cin discussed the merits of food plants, Mac told Bry about the group that climbed to the gorge and met a mountain lion...

Morning: the Crum spilled out of the burrow early, everyone finding it very crowded in the small space. Roo reminded himself that this year he needed to start on a lower level for nest bed places. Outside they found Dre laughing, "You all look like ants escaping a wrecked hill!" He was above the seating stones sitting on a mossy root. Cor laughed too. With mock affront she said, "Very funny! It's a little close in there." She joined him on the root. She found that Dre looked years younger, healthier, and radiating a new calm confidence.

"You know I told them about you, and it was a minor uproar that they never knew that part of our history. Mostly they feel sorry for your loss and happy to know that you are found again."

She thought, "Are you happy, too?" and Dre smiled, answering, "I am, Roo is good to me, and we've found a good routine. As I can't talk to the animals, I can't take any watch duties, so I help with the food gathering. Lately I've been working on Pip's boat, though I hope no harm comes to anyone who rides on it. I know you are enjoying your freedom from leadership, I'm glad for you."

"Yes, it's wonderful to be free, riding on Weh away from everyone, though Hep misses the old me always being close to him at the burrow. He is fine, he sends his good thoughts and a hug."

Mar and Par made a tentative move to join them, and Cor introduced the two females. Dre smiled at them, "There were twins in my mountain clan too, a female and a male, about my age." Dre didn't need to hear their thoughts to feel the sympathy from them, it was all over their faces. "It's okay, I'm happy here, now, and It is wonderful to meet such pretty Crum." Matching blushes and smiles rewarded Dre. "Yes, I will teach you to swim."

Cor chuckled at the retreating younglings, "That was funny. It must have been right there on top of their minds."

"Not very nice of me but I think I'll enjoy spending time with them, they are young and that's an amazing gift to me at my age, to see the world through their eyes."

Tym and Tyl came up next and Cor left the three as introductions were made.

Roo braced the burrow door closed and joined the entire party laughing and talking as they walked to the boat. It was a beautiful sunny day, warm and cloudless after several days of spring rain. Today they would be swimming and viewing the progress on Pips boat. The winter waves had pushed up sand to make a beach in the curve of the river, the dune crowned with the upside-down wood boat. This was where the Crum set out the food baskets and blankets. Roo took a watch post on the nearest tree, he'd trade with Bry at noon.

Par pushed through the waist deep water to where Dre stood waiting. Pip had given the basic instructions to the whole group while on the beach but now the new students had to get in and swim. Tym was working with his brother, Pip with Mar and Mac helping Bry. The rest cheered them on and threw jokes from the sand or sitting on the boat. Mar and Par had a natural grace, floating and stroking thin limbs through the water like minnows. Til went at the craft like he was chopping wood, determined with lots of noise and splashing, eventually finding a rhythm that kept him afloat. Bry was hopeless, he flayed his arms and forgot to kick, kicked like mad and didn't remember to stroke, swallowing river water and giving the audience a dramatic comedy. Par swam circles around him just to tease the old Crum.

Cor and Cin had decided that they didn't need to learn swimming that bad and stayed in the shallows with Cra and Kam.

After a wonderful meal of chopped greens dressed in oil and honey and snails and walnuts the Crum all took a hold of the boat and turned it over. Lis finally committed herself to the trip, telling Pip that she would go with him when he went. The two brothers would go too. Par was yelling, "Me too!" and every Crum there yelled back, "No, you won't!" Dre was laughing from the rocks above them, he knew that Par was determined to go on the adventure.

Til stayed behind at North Burrow, he would go on the boat. Bry and Cin stayed, they had said goodbye to everyone before they came and considered the North Burrow their new home. Cor and Jmy had to drag the twins away, they wanted to stay longer. The two-week visit had flashed by. Tich was again burdened with baskets, now filled with raw and salted rodent skins, salt, pine nuts, lily bulbs and snails' shells. Weh had parted from her father and his new brood, grateful for the visit but wanting to get home to the den at Home Tree. Her baskets were lighter, she would carry the Crum back packs as well as Cor and Jmy.

CHAPTER TWELVE

THE BOAT AND CONSEQUENCES

They had six long spear-shaped oars, and the entire boat was planned smooth and buffed with beeswax from its pointed bow to rounded stern. It was mostly flat bottomed with rounded curved sides reaching as high as a sitting Crum's waist. Four bench seats had been carved from the wood and that was where the travellers would sit. Hemp made ropes were looped through holes along the rail edges to hold down the packs of food, tied loops holding snail shells and provide hand holds for the Crum passengers. In the stern was a large stone, ridged, to hold the very long rope attached to it, an anchor. When all was ready the boat was dragged to the river's shallows wear it rocked until the sailing Crum climbed aboard. Pip and Lis at the front benches, Til and Tym behind them. Dre, Roo and Bry pushed the stern into the flow until it lifted and was caught by the current. The onlookers watched, frightened and excited as the Crum aboard scrambled to dip oars and try to control the boat. Cra gasped when the boat tilted with Pips weight when he leaned out to grab a dropped oar. Lis was rocked into Tym and they both hurriedly reset themselves to balance on the benches. Til's heart gave a lurch, grabbed at the rail, suddenly feeling helpless to control anything. Pip yelled for them to raise the oars out of the water, to sit still and let the boat steady itself. It smoothed out and found the centre current, taking them downriver without needing guidance.

After watching the departing adventurers, Cra and Roo slowly moved into the forest to Ryks place. The four kits were half grown and almost weaned, two were up trees and one pushing into her mother's stomach. Another was on top of Ryks head, hands almost covering his squinting eyes. At their approach he unceremoniously dumped his prodigy into the dirt and shook his self, blinking eyes at them. "He is gone now on his boat?"

"Yes, they looked shaky until they got into the centre of the river then they just floated away downstream." Roo answered the raccoon.

Cra kept silent, looking miserable. Ryk, wanting to change the subject, said, "We've given them names. This one is Pip." he nose-pointed to the one he had dumped that was now halfway up a tree. That one is Bop, and that is Boo pushing Bop out of the tree and little Pik with his mother. The mother in question, Ine, said, "I'll be glad when they are done nursing and start foraging for themselves. "They are exhausting!"

Roo set to work on the digging out a second level under the burrow. They placed the descending hole near the back of the burrow after finding the soil deep and rock free there. Because his talented young wood workers were gone, it was decided that Blue and himself to be the wood cutters and shapers and it was Bry and Mac and who did the digging out, with Cra, Kam and Dre removing the buckets of dirt. They slanted the tunnel until it was to the depth of two standing Crums below the upper floor before moving sideways to make sleeping alcoves. All of it needed shoring up, steps and ladders made. The older Crum remembered working just this way in the Home Tree burrow to expand the rooms there and had to laugh at the irony of doing a young Crum's work when they could have stayed in comfort at the Home Burrow. They were relieved when it was their turn on watch duty or to gather food as the work was all consuming.

It was twilight, a week after they had gone, when Acky dropped onto Roo's watch branch.

"We haven't seen them, sorry, we lost track of them at the gorge when my cousin crow was attacked by an eagle there. When he could go back, they must have entered under a forest canopy. But we will keep looking, sorry. "Roo thanked him, it wasn't his fault, he had to trust that they would get out of any trouble they would find themselves in.

For Pip the trouble started just before the gorge. They got distracted by the eagle's fight with a crow and missed the jutting rocks barely cresting the water's surface. The ride had been easy until then, they had relaxed and watched the forest stream passed. Astonished when the gorges white water was there already, the many days walk reduced to a couple of hours. They hit the rock with a shuddering crack and a hole was opened between the wood grains. Water seeped in, Tym hurriedly untied a snail shell that had been hung on the side ropes and began bailing water. The boat had slewed sideways with the impact and the frothing water was pushing it to a dipping angle. They threw their weight to the high side and dipped in the oars to turn the stern forward again. The water sped up with the added gush from the gorge outflow and they were moving faster into the northern curve of the river, the last place seen when they had met the lion. The boat pushed against the high bank of the bend. They could see into a mixed forest, the evergreen trees interspersed with more deciduous, a startled deer ogled from the trees. The vessel almost upended as it scraped the rocky edge and Tym went overboard, managing to grasp the rope ties and stay with the boat. Afraid to tilt the boat, Pip and Lis put their weight to the opposite side so Til could help get his brother back onboard. They twirled in the fast eddy, the boat spinning like a dry leaf, but it was no longer dry, the bottom was filling, past their ankles now.

Tym's arm had twisted, and he pushed it under his shirt to immobilize it while the other hand swept the shell through the rising boat water. Liz and Pip were pushing the oars through the current, trying to control or slow the boat. By holding the oar fluke flat on against the water he found it made a small brake. He yelled this to Lis and they both worked to steady and slow the craft. Til had an idea, he opened one of the packs and pulled out a pine nut. With a knife from his side pouch, he cut it into slivers and stuffed them into the crack, then stamped his booted foot on the hole to hold the mushed nut meat in place. That slowed the leak to a trickle, but it meant he had to stay that way with his body angled awkwardly while working with the oar. He left off trying to row and started helping his brother in the bailing, the water was now at shin level and soaked through the bottom of the backpacks.

If they had time to look, they would have seen the mostly flat land, full of low brush and large leave trees: maples, oaks, birch, ash and beech. The river widened and slowed a little on its own. Pip and Lis set down the oars and looked at the brothers behind them. Til smiled and pointed at his foot; the boot toe now just covered with the last of the water. "I've slowed it for now but I'm afraid to move my foot least my plug pops out."

Pip asked Tym how his arm was. "It hurts but not broken." He took it out of his shirt and slowly unbent it and flexed his hand. "It will be okay by tomorrow."

That was when they realized that the sun had sunk to the treetops, they were hungry and still moving, now going northwest.

After a meal of nuts and fruit they traded places, Lis and Pip in the back with Pip taking a turn at keeping the plug secured. They replaced the nut meat with a slim wood wedge carved off a bench but still didn't trust it though they thought the wood would swell to fit more snuggly after a while. That done they discussed trying for the bank on the left. The sun set and they chose to stay on board, feeling safer away from an unknown forest that could be governed by unfriendly predators. It was a fateful decision, one made by exhausted minds lulled by the peaceful river.

Lis woke first, pushing her Shum off her head and tucking the front of the Shum up to free her arms. She gasped, whipping her head around and saw no forest, no land. Her cry woke the others. "Oh no! We must have flowed into a lake, a big one! Pip cried, full of dismay. How would they find a shore? The boat rocked gently, and they could feel it move slowly in a current, westerly. There began the time of trial for the four sailors, they couldn't move the vessel faster than they were already moving, couldn't control its direction, and had limited food.

The first night on the lake, the crew were enthralled with the unfettered vault of sky, billions of stars, and a tiny sliver of moon.

The second day they rationed the food and covered their heads with the shums, the unrelenting sun more that they had ever experienced having lived always under tree cover.

The third day a storm came, the wind pushed waves against the rocking sides and the heavy rain beat on their hunched backs and filled the boat with more water. They worked to stay in the craft, to bailed out the rain and keep warm in the new chill. That night there were no stars, and they had no appetite, a good thing because they had only two sad little pine nuts left.

Pip dreamed that Cra was shaking him but what he heard from her mouth was a squawk. Another loader squawk came just has he felt the boat shudder. A seagull had dropped out of the sun to pulled at one of the tied packs, luckily still secured to the rope at the rails. It flapped furiously thinking, "Mine! What? Stuck! Mine-mine-mine!" Lis and Tym pulled their spears from their backs and stabbed at the large bird until it let go. The good news was that they had bumped onto a gravel beach.

Pip jumped to the ground but was surprised that that his knees were so shaky that he knelt, holding to the rail for support. Til and Tym had the same reaction, Lis stayed aboard long enough to untie their packs and throw them onto the beach. She looked around at their now tilted vessel, picked up the anchor and chucked it overboard as a last act of defiance before getting out with Tyms help, who was standing easier now. They faced the forest crowding the beach and knew that was where they had to go. Familiar food and shelter of some kind lay there, they needed to recover and look to find the way home. Supporting each other like two sets of new-born rats they went to the first patch of soft ground, chucked aside a matt of last year's leaves, and dug out four grubs. Too hungry to wash them first, they got a cursory swipe on clothes before being eaten.

Pip looked at his companions. Dirty, grey faces sunburned and thinner, smelly leather clothes in need of mending and washing, as well as their bodies although he was immune to the smell now. They smiled at each other and began to laugh with the sheer joy of being off the water and under a tree canopy. A squirrel up a nearby tree thought that were the most interesting things he had ever seen but he couldn't see what was so funny.

They ate a little more, then opened their packs, pulled out a set of musty damp clothes, returned to the lake to lay them over the boat sides to air, undressed and stepped into the water to wash and drink, though the lake had a fishy taste to it. At noon they moved into the trees, spears in hand, back packs stuffed with the rinsed old clothes.

Too weak for climbing they made a shelter under a raised tree root backed by a clot of tree detritus. Safe at least on three sides they were asleep before twilight, wrapped in dirty but warm shums.

Slowly they became stronger after finding and enjoying fresh rainwater in a still pool, bright green fern shoots, tree snails and amazingly a berry feast of tart cranberries. They stuffed their packs with the berries but were not worried so much about finding food now that they were in the familiar flora.

The second day in the new forest they saw a herd of small deer, but they weren't interested in making conversation, ghosting out of site almost as soon as they were spotted.

The third day it was a ferocious ill-tempered skunk who chased them up a tree, depositing a terrible spray against its bark. They had to sleep that night in the tree, finally crossing over to the next tree on touching branches like squirrels. The mother and her brood eventually departed, black and white tails waving superior goodbyes.

Two more days of uneventful southwest traveling through rich dense woodland meeting only the critters their size or smaller, squirrels, chipmunks, mice, birds, and a shy clutch of rabbits; then their path was crossed by a stream.

They could easily cross it on the exposed rocks, its bubbling gurgle reminding them of Home Tree's creek, only a little smaller. They had to decide, should they continue the direction they were going to or follow this as it might be emptying into the river at North Burrow? If they came to the river, the same problem applied, how to get across. The original idea was to find Dubs gradual zigzag route up to the level of the escarpment and down the leaning tree. It was the yearning for the familiar river that had them turning to follow the stream south. When they came upon a young beaver and asked where the stream went, he replied, "big fast water" they took that to mean their river and left him to his chewed branches and attempts at damming the creek. With lighter hearts they hurried their steps south to the river, they would figure it all out from there, maybe they could look across at the burrow!

CHAPTER THIRTEEN
THE LEGACY OF DUB

Dub came to visit the burrow and saw Blu on watch in the hemlock and Dre coming out the doorway. Slabs of wood and shavings were leaning on stones near the door, a mound of flat stones beside it. No one else was in sight and that surprised him, the Crum usually spent all their daylight time outside. Dre set down his buckets of dirt and went back inside to tell the workers that the Bear was back. The Crum all spilled out of the burrow, in various degrees of dirt coating, Mac and Bry so coated they looked entirely brown. Dub laughed and hopped, making the more skittish birds take flight.

"What you doing? Making holes in ground?"

Roos smile was bright against the soil smudges. "Exactly! We are making a new lower level to expand the burrow for more Crum."

"Ya, more Crum!" He looked over them, trying to remember the identities under the dirt. "No twin young?"

"No, they went back to the Home Burrow. Dub have you seen Pip? Lis, Tym and Til? They took a boat ride down the river almost two weeks ago. They were expecting to come back through the way you travel, up the escarpment."

"Oh! That way is the Big water, Big-big water."

"You mean a lake?"

Cra abruptly sat down on the ground. Kam moved to sit beside her to place her hand on her shoulder.

"Ya, maybe they get out before, good forest there but has wolves. I no go there."

"Wolves? There is a wolf pack there?"

Dub nodded, "I go pee." He proceeded to follow his usual routine of setting his scent marks around the hemlock then up and down the hill. Raccoons and foxes scattered or climbed trees at his approach, making him laugh at the hullabaloo he caused. Roo followed him, full of worry now, it was things he never expected Pip and his group to have to deal with, what if he made it to the lake? Dub made it sound like it was much bigger than Dres' Mountain Lake, something he could barely imagine. Dub stopped to look in the black wolfs crevasse, the bottom now had only bones and some scatter of black hair amongst the dry willow stems.

"Dub, are they friendly wolves? Do you communicate with them?"

"Wolves are not good or bad. They have their place. I have my place. We don't cross. I stay away." Dub ambled back to the burrow to cross the water there. Before he left, he said he would watch at the edge of the wolf's territory for Pips group.

They could see the river through an almost solid mesh of leaves, the stream did empty into the river, but they didn't recognize where they were along its course. The trees had gradually transitioned into the fir trees they had expected, as well as land with its shield rocks and hills slanting towards the river, so they knew they had to be closer to the burrow. Moving back into the forest proper they continued southwest and were finally rewarded with the sight of the gorge spilling its fury into the flow across from them.

Feeling safer but less comfortable, they spent the nights up in trees, finding crooks and abandoned nests and even once an owl roost. They were woken the one morning by a scuffling fight and canine giggles just under the pine tree they were sleeping in. Wolf pups, three of them, all round and clumsy, nipped at ears and tails, yipping gleefully. Pip could count at least fifteen adults all around him, prowling or laying around or chewing at old bones.

If they made some movement in the tree, they might be assumed to be squirrels and be ignored; if they got down to the ground, they would for sure be seen and probably chewed on a bit. The Crum checked for branches that crossed into other trees and seeing it was possible they climbed and scampered ungracefully on to the next tree's limb, and sure enough, they caught the attention of the mother wolf and soon all the other wolves were looking at them in curiosity.

One of the big males said, "That's the ugliest squirrels I ever saw."

Another said, "I don't think they are squirrels, no tails." The pups asked if they could eat them, and the mother said you'd have to get them out of the tree.

Pip had nothing lose, so he sat down on the limb he was hanging from and addressed the audience; "We are Crum, we taste terrible so don't try to eat us. We are trying to get back to our home across the river."

Nonplussed, the mother wolf said, "You can hear us, how strange. How did you get here if you were over there?"

"I can tell you the story, but we would like to get out of this tree."

The Crum halted their climb down just out of reach of the pups and waited, fingers and boot toes stuck in the bark notches. While they waited, they looked from the mother to her too-close grinning prodigy. Finally, she laughed and cuffed them away, telling them to find other playthings.

When all four were on the needle coated earth, they bowed to the wolves and that made them smile. Several laid down close by, a few stayed standing but in a what looked like a normal guarded awareness. Pip told the story, with the others coming in with their parts: from the beginning at Home Tree to the move to North burrow and finally to the boat ride (Interrupted by questions and explanations to what was a boat) floating down the river. When they told of how they ended up in the lake, there was a great stir amongst the pack. "You were on the great water!" This earned them a degree of new respect. It became apparent that this land was all the wolf packs territory and they had got away with not being found before now by sheer luck. The pack had been away, hunting for the deer herd.

Pip asked, with as much politeness as he could, if they could drink some water and eat a little. The pack turned at once and silently moved through the forest to a large pool. On its glassy surface was the reflection of a low den opening set into a huge rock jumble above. The Crum had to jog fast to keep up. When they fell panting to their knees at the water to drink, the pack moved into the family business of feeding the pups, eating more of a deer carcass, relaxing on the warm rocks, and keeping guard.

They were watched, of course, but Pips group felt relaxed enough to get on with the digging up and washing of food and the cutting of fresh leaves from a wild ginger to eat from and then to eat. The afternoon passed with no move towards the Crum. The wolves seem to have accepted their presence. Finally, Pip went to the female matriarch that all the wolves seemed to defer to.

"We would like to get back to our home, would you allow us to move through your land?"

"How did you expect to cross river? We are stopped by water."

"A long time ago my friend Roo and I came to the Great Falls and there we met a bear named Dub. Last year he needed help, so he took us on his back through an aspen forest and on a slow trek through the descending woodland until he was level with the river. Then he swam across the water to the burrow. He knew where it was because a wolverine used to live there. Our trip home was to follow the way he had gone up to the top of the falls. It's possible to cross the river up there on a tree bridge. From there we climb down the escarpment on a tree that has fallen onto the rock cliff wall. That's how we get back."

"Hmm. I see. We know Dub. We do not cross into his place, he doesn't come into ours, this way we have peace and food plenty. You sleep here tonight. I send two of my young to take you to bears land." This spoken, she closed her piercing yellow eyes and ignored Pip.

The night was spent on the ground, they figured that they were safe now, if the wolves wanted to hurt them, they would have by now. It was between two upraised roots of a tree that they made a bed; the deep vee secured them on either side if not from above. Since the storm on the lake, it hadn't rained though the air felt denser today. Curling into their shums, they listened to the songs of the wolf pack, the lonely howls at a fat moon.

"Maybe they lied. Maybe they really are good to eat!" The Crum woke to the prodding and sniffing of cold wet noses belonging to three cheerful squirming pups all trying to get close, bumping chubby bodies in a tussle. Lis pushed at a nose and laughingly said, "Ewwee, wolf snot!" and made a show of wiping her hand on her shum. That had the three giggling and rolling; but it allowed the Crum to get out from between the tree roots.

They washed and breakfasted until two sleek young females came to them. "We go now." Said the larger one. I go here, you climb. I take two." She moved against the nearest tree and stood against it. Pip and Lis were quickly seated on the wolves back, Til and Tym on the other female. They had just time to grab on the neck and back fur before they were slipping through the forest with such grace and efficiency that Pip couldn't help but compare the rolling gait of his raccoon to this splendid animal. "Thank you." Said the wolf. "You ride raccoon, we eat raccoon. Funny."

"We eat small fish, grubs, snails but no one bigger. We do kill the rats and mice for our making of clothes, our animal friends eat the bodies."

"I eat that too, but I prefer big juicy raccoon." Now the Crum figured the wolf was teasing them. "Don't worry, we won't hunt until we leave you at bear land."

With that she dropped into alert travel thinking, noting everything that she passed, aware of every creature around her. The two transported their charges over large swathes of land that would have taken the Crum days to cover, until stopping suddenly at a giant mother tree, a white pine almost has big as Home Tree. The wolf smelled around the bottom of the tree and pushed his back on it. "You are here, I go home." The action was repeated by the other animal. When on the ground, the Crum bowed to their rides, but they barely received a nod before they were gone, disappearing into the tree shadows.

Not knowing Dubs present location, the four Crum set off uphill, though Pip didn't yet recognize this woodland yet, he knew that he needed a way up, to the top of the escarpment. When they came upon the gravel bank, Pip knew where he was at, he found bear scat and then, on the well-travelled path up the zigzag, traces of brown fur smelling of Dub. Sleeping in another tree that night, Til and Tym wished for a ride home, wished for their own nest beds. Lis added that she never wanted to sleep in a tree again. Pip told them about his trip he went on when he was their age, the one where he met Ryk. "I spent a very comfortable night in a woodpecker's hollow in a tree; it was full of old feathers. But I might be tougher than you three!" They smiled, knowing he wasn't serious. Pip was very proud of them; this was the first complaints they had voiced and only spoken now that they could visualize getting back to the burrow soon.

The next afternoon was overcast when they entered the aspen grove with its round rattling leaves, pale grey trunks and a million bird residents. The birds fell quiet, and the leaves turned to flash their white undersides with a quickening wind. Looking for a place to shelter, Pip came around a large boulder and saw the top of a bear in the distance behind a hedge of vines. They were overjoyed, that must be Dub! They could see he was eating something. Just about to call out, they were shocked to see another bear, the real Dub, come barrelling towards it, roaring with fury. The smooth aspen trunks were difficult to get up and Pip couldn't recall how he got up in the branches, all he had thoughts for was that one of the combatants was Dub, defending his land. They witnessed the most terrible fight, horrible to behold, all frightening roars, rending claws and tearing teeth. Dub was delt slashes across his face, ripping furrows over forehead and eye. The other bear lost an ear and had a deep rip in his side. They rolled and rent and finally the stranger bear limped away, bleeding heavily.

Dub stood swaying then dropped heavily to the ground. The Crum climbed down, falling half the way in their hurry to get to their friend.

"Dub, you are hurt! What can we do?!" cried Pip. It started to rain, and the bear lifted his bleeding face to the shower.

"Hello Pip. I bad. You can't help. I hurt bad." Dub turned his neck to show them a deep bite at his neck with a steady flow of blood seeping out of him, soaking through the dark fur and onto the ground. Horrified and shocked, the Crum cried and stayed by the dying bear. All they could do was tell him how brave and wonderful he was, that they would tell his story to everyone, forever. It didn't take long before his body ceased to move. The rain stopped; the clouds parted revealing a last spear of the setting light to fall on the still tableau. Pip thought how he'd never forget this moment, how softly the sun touched the shiny fur, how much a loss he felt.

They spent the night by the river, too tired and unhappy to climb into a tree but finding a good shelter in an old unused raccoon den. Its previous dweller was probably dispatched by Dub long ago. Barring any new calamity, tomorrow they would cross the tree bridge, go down the leaning tree and be back to the burrow at the end of the day.

All the birds had spread the word of the great bear fight, Acky had brought the news that one of the bears had died but nothing came to them about the travellers. Roo and Cra asked their old friends, Fen and Ryk to take them to the falls. They had to know how Dub was, and if he needed help. Cra held on to the hope that her brother and friends were on their way back, maybe even close by. Fen took Roo with Ryk and Cra trailing behind, the raccoon, rounder and slower these days. While he rode Roo asked after the other foxes in his den and what was new in the forest, explaining: "I haven't been far from the burrow, but that job is almost finished now."

Fen said he was glad to get away, the kits were forever wanting to play or hunt or eat absolutely anything. "The woods are quiet; the news of the bear fight has the animals wondering what will happen next."

They crossed the home tree creek and dismounted before the brush, thanking their two friends for the rides, and that they didn't know how long they would be. Ryk and Fen wanted to stay in the area for a while to hunt and see what was new, delaying having to go back to the responsibility of parenting.

Roo and Cra moved through the bushes to the leaning tree only to see it shake with descending Crum. "Ha! All I can see is dirty butts coming down!" Roo called up, laughing with pure joy and relief. Cra cried and laughed and when they were down, hugged them all, telling them they really stank. After hugging his best friend, Roo asked how Dub was. Pips face fell and he quietly told him that their friend had died from the terrible and frightening fight with another bear. "I think the new bear will have died too; it had a big hole in his side. It had moved away into the Aspens and Pines." Roo was shaken, he turned away to face the falls. Cra came to his side and said, "Let's go see." Roo, red eyed but calm, told Pip that Fen and Ryk were close by at the creek, and they could probably ask for a ride back. He and Cra were going to see Dub.

Pip pushed through the bushes with Lis and the brothers following to see Ryks behind and bushy tail in the air, waving, his head emersed in the creek as he fished for the spill of river trout. Across the stream was Fen, pouncing on a tempting frog. The Crum laughed, and two wet faces turned to grinned at them. "What took you so long?!" asked Ryk.

Cra had never been up the escarpment. She was enthralled at the amazing view from the tree bridge and stood watching the vast sky dotted with clouds paint shadows here and there on the forest below. Roo took her hand and together they moved to the aspen grove where they found their friends body, his spirit free now to laugh at the earth below. Roo wanted to be sure of the other bear and if it had really died. They followed the blood trail until they found it, dead also in a slump under the low boughs of a pine. They didn't linger there, the area suddenly felt chill and unwelcoming.

The bob cats rumbling purr vibrated against Mars back as she leaned back on the warm fur. She clutched her knees and drew her shum over her whole body. The day had a chill, winter was coming. They were in the Home Tree Forest, near Tichs new den, close to the tree he enjoyed scouting from. Mar would always think of Win in relation to this tree. Her life seemed to begin on the fateful day of her Dedas injury and Wins passing. Before that her days seemed childish and very mundane. Tich was catnapping, occasionally stretching out his claws in rhythmic flexes.

She thought she could be a healer like Cra. It was time to declare her adult trade and more than anything she wanted to go back the North Burrow. Par would go too; her sister was born a hunter. She would miss her parents, but the call of the wild north was in her now, she could hardly wait until the spring.

Mar lifted her face to the wind rustling leaves, all golden and russets and soft umber browns behind dove-grey skies. The curled bobcat tucked under his paws and settled into a deeper dose.

BOOK TWO-CHAPTER FOURTEEN

CRUMS OF CHANGE

Ten years have passed since Roo brought his friends north to establish a home in a burrow under an old hemlock tree. The small group of Crum have lived in (mostly) harmony with the help of the local animals, swelling in Crum population every summer with students from the two other burrows to the south and southwest. But nothing stays the same in nature, it's always evolving, our world of change.

The North Burrow Crum had awakened from their hibernation with the spring sap coursing through the hemlock tree, the joyous renewing that comes with the suns gift. Throwing open the doors and exiting the burrow always felt like a new birth, a reacquaintance with the forest and their animal friends. From the trees high rock shelf, the view of the fast smooth river was steel grey, blanketed with a low early fog. There was a crisp bite to the early air, but its fresh clean smell was invigorating after the long sleep. Pine needles glistened with dew and the tweeting clatter of bird song greeted the emerging Crum.

When Roo's fox didn't come to see him this morning, Roo and Cra went in search of him, up the rock slope, feeling a stretch to their cramped legs. They had left the rest of the burrow's habitants moving around or sitting on the landing's seating stones, eating the first meal of grubs and new green sprouts. Cra and Roo stood in front of Fen outside his den as he lay in a wonderful ray of warmth coming through the fir needled boughs. Roo was startled to see the changes, unnoticed before on his friend. The elder Fox was sleeping, his soft snores puffing out his whiskers with each exhalation. It seemed to happen too quickly this aging, the foxes muzzle whitening and the bony haunches poking through thin fur. The other fox, his mate, Mai, sat curled next to Fen, slitted golden eyes watchful but friendly. Roo stroked Fens red and white cheek fur, remembered the youthful carelessness though bright perfect days, hunting for rodents, fur, and food. Roo put his face in Fens big ear and yelled, "Wake up old fox!" and laughed as the animal yipped and shook his head vigorously, glaring at the two smiling Crum. "I got tired of waiting for you lazy Crum to finally emerge from your hole!", Fen grouched and yawned showing an impressive set of sharp yellow teeth. Mai hmphed in derision and retreated into the forest, parting the heads of bright trilliums that dotted this section of the woods. Their kits had all moved on, all but one and Mai would join her in hunting for their breakfast. Roo told him, "Now that I see you are alright, I'll see you later. I must talk to the others and clean up the burrow." Roo and Cra turned to go but Fen stopped them with the unwelcome news that Ryk, the raccoon friend of Pips, was missing. "Oh no!" said Cra, her sienna-coloured eyes widening. "Thank you for telling us, we will see Pip now, at the burrow." The fox watched the two mated Crum go, bumping shoulders and heads close. Roo, a head taller than his mate, their camouflaging cloaks swishing over their backs.

Spring had swollen the river, its relentless passage licking and swallowing its banks, pushing debris and jetsam past Pip as he sat on a high waterside rock. The Crum's straight leaf-coloured hair flopped over his face and brow and Pip swatted it back, away from eyes. Pip was stocky and heavily muscled from pulling at fishing nets and carving on logs. He stared unseeing at the water, wide and fast while the mild morning sun warmed his shoulders and leather clothed body. Suddenly in front of his face was the head of a river otter, sun sparkling on the too close face. "Hi! It said cheerfully and then grinned at Pip. Exasperated, Pip pushed the strange otter away. "Go! Would you!" The otter wiggled up next to Pips rock, swinging its long body and tail out of the stream. It sighed and crossed its front paws. "What matter?" It finally asked. Pip stayed quiet until the Otter nudged his elbow with its head, snuggling close against Pip. "My raccoon friend is gone; I'm thinking he left the forest this winter and he either got himself ate or he died far away. He was getting kind of old." said Pip The otter said, "Ahhh!" With great sympathy and laid its head across Pips lap, taking up the entire front of Pip's legs. "Geees, get off!" and pushed the wet head off, muttering, "Fish breath." The river animal slipped again into the water right in front of the Crum so Pip couldn't help but react to the warm brown eyes and funny whiskered face. Quickly it went through a series of face-making. Scrunching his face tiny then opening his eyes wide, blinking, and grinning then bobbing his head. Pip just had to laugh at its silliness and the otter laughed with him. "I Bob!" he said and proceeded to bob his head in demonstration.

"Okay, I'm Pip. Thanks for cheering me up. You belong to the otter family." Pip waved downstream. Bob bobbed. "Mother tell me go, she had new pups. I come here. I be a friend." "Well, you are no raccoon but at least you can fish, and I like fishing." Pip told him. "But now I must join my group, my sister needs someone to boss about. "Pip got to his feet and moved into the pines, walking parallel to the river, toward the North Burrow tree.

He met Roo and Cra as they were leaving the fox den, waving to Fen, and walking with them to the burrow, the slanting ground full of pushing green shoots spreading the matt of thick rust-coloured needles. "Ryk is missing, his mate told me he left to find a meal and never came back. Pip paused then added, "I feel like my youth is going out with our animals." Roo placed a hand on Pips shum clad shoulder in sympathy.

They were met by the twins, Mar and Par as they walked near the hemlocks upper root base. The two young females were considered adults now, both beautiful and entirely opposite. Mar, the healer, wore her dark green hair in a loose fall over her back where Par, the hunter had tied and braided hers to keep it out of the way of her stone-tipped spear. "They are all here now, we've left you some food."

The five of them joined the other seated Crum, enjoying the first meal after waking from the winter's hibernation. They sat on two circles of stones on the burrow's large entry landing with its gentle waterfall behind them, it's source far up the hill:

its destination, the great river that passed just below the high bank. The burrow door was choked open to air out the rooms, the Crum-sized opening was flanked by two great stones that snugged against the tree bark. The burrow went under the hemlock's roots in the space between the ledge of rock and the lower set of tree roots delving deep into the ground below.

These were the permanent settlers; the numbers would grow with summer students and visitors bringing welcome news and supplies not found in the coniferous forest. There was one Crum seated outside the circle of residents, but they included Dre in all their conversations and meals. He had spent the winter sleep in the burrow but would now move back into his old shelter up the hill near a patch of lilies. The rest of the Crum varied from the oldest, Cin and Bry, both near two hundred years to the young pretty twins. Their trades were a necessary mix of hunters, weavers, stone cutters, and gatherers. It was a far less number compared to Home Tree's burrow of hundred or more.

Roo swept his hands through his wild curls, flashed a tentative smile at the assembly, said to everyone: "Pip tells me that Ryk is gone, Fen is okay, he was sleeping in the sun. Were there any other changes over the winter?" Roo's bright eyes scanned the group. They all had been stretching their legs while filling the food baskets for the first meal. A chorus of sympathetic murmurs were aimed at Pip.

Just then Roo was distracted by a river otter bobbing out of the river, close by the waters bank. Roo asked, "What's it doing?" to no one in particular. The otter was going through its repertoire of faces and bobs, making everyone laugh. Pip told them, "That's just Bob, I met him down the river. By the way, another big log has washed up on the beach curve, even bigger than the last one." Bob grinned and moved onto the shore closer to Pip. "I think Bob has adopted me."

The brothers, Tym and Til looked at Lis and they all looked at Pip. They had all been on the near fatal boat ride previously and were wondering if they could improve on the experience.

Par waited until everyone reported their findings amongst the forest's animals and new food discoveries before she told them about Tich's news. "Our bobcat has found a mate, Chi. They have a new den by the great falls. Between the two of them, they have claimed that area has theirs. They will spend less time near us at the burrow. Being they are top predators they will hunt farthest from our protected friends around here. He has seen signs of Lon, our mountain lion, closer to us now. Tich thinks that without our bear, the cat has taken this area under his protection. That's another reason for Tich and Chi to stay away from here." There were nods all around. After Dub's horrible death, the North Burrow Crum were afraid that a less amiable stranger would menace this part of the forest. Cra said what they all had been thinking, "We have been lucky these few years that no one has moved here. Without his scent markings we are open to any large new animal."

"That's only because they have been afraid of me!" It was the bobcats, Tich and Chi, coming through the trees to join the group. Tich was a fully grown, standing at least two and a half feet at his thickly muscled shoulders. Chi was slightly smaller and slimmer, with dun-coloured spotted fur and bright hazel eyes. "Welcome, Chi! How can you put up with this flea-bitten bag of wind?" teased white-haired Bry, grinning at Chi. The female cat's eyes widened at the new experience of Crum words in her head, while hearing deep chirping coming from the leather clad creatures. She smiled and narrowed her eyes then at her mate, Tich. "Don't worry, I know both his good strengths and his faults." Loving the teasing that Tich was enduring, all the Crum laughed when Tich bowed to her in subservience. "There has been some wolves and a badger that we chased away this winter. All is quiet now." With this report and introduction, Tich and Chi left the Crum, returning the way they had come to their home several miles to the west, closer to the great waterfall.

The crow had been waiting for the cats to depart before fluttering down to set on the rock ledge above the seating stones. It was Acky with news from Home Tree, the large burrow to the southwest. "They will come here at the new moon." Lis threw the bird a grub from their food baskets before Acky took off.

The spring clean-up began. All the nest beds needed their furs aired and grasses replaced. The food pantry needed refilling with fresh greens and washed grubs, the main staple of Crum diet. They would have to wait a while for the berries to come in, but new shoots of dandelions and ferns were plentiful and easily harvested. Cra and Mar, were treating a trickle of hurt animals that came up to the Make-Well back door. They would take care of these animals before going into the forest to check on the populations of rabbits, hares, raccoons, squirrels, and other smaller denizens under their protection. Pip and Dre went fishing for the small fry that they would dump into the pantry's freshwater trough. Bob joined them but was more hindrance than help, at least he kept them amused.

As the leader, Roo made up a watch list schedule on a piece of paper-birch bark with sharpened charcoal. Everyone but Cin and Dre took turns to man the branch of the hemlock that overlooked the woods. Cin was excluded because of her age; Dre because of his inability to talk to intruders. Once the list was hung in the burrow common room, Roo would take the first watch himself.

Roo looked over the north burrow forest. Where his old home was mostly level with a mix of deciduous trees: maples, oaks, and birches with only the occasional pine, here was a piney forest marching down the slope to the wide fast river. The acidic needles and sun blocking treetops kept down heavy undergrowth amongst the boulder strewn woods. Dusty rays of sunlight shot down through the canopy, dabbling the dim forest with many joyful oases of colour. He was distracted by the caws and squarks of three crows chasing away a raven, the smaller birds of the forest quietly watching the by-play. Raven dispatched, the birdsong and animal clatter resumed. Crum worked around and below his post halfway up the tree, chatting to each other and to the animals as they cheerfully worked. Roo looked west, upriver towards the escarpment and thought that he'd been neglecting to go there, the death of the two bears too painful. It was also the only way for Crum to get to the other side of the river. "I've let my grief stop me. This year I'll have to go up there, maybe take my students. Sooner than that, though, I need to go east up into Lon's territory, to thank Lon for looking after this land for us."

CHAPTER FIFTEEN

DANGER AT THE GORGE

The next morning, with their safety from predators foremost on his mind, Roo proposed to take the trip of several days to the high gorge where Lon had a den nearby. This had to be accomplished before the visitors arrived from Home Tree and South Burrow, a few weeks away. Cra wanted to join him as well as the two brothers, Til and Tym. Til was the oldest and taller, both had warm brown eyes the colour of Bella mushroom caps and short scruffy hair. Mar was left in charge of the Make-Well healing work; Dre, Blu, Mac, Kam, Pip and Bry could handle any emergencies that might come up. They would walk instead of riding any of their friends: fox, rabbit, or raccoon. It would not do to deliver them as possible meals to the mountain lion. They all carried spears and warning pipes, backpacks with useful tools, water bottles and medical supplies (Cra never went anywhere without it). Til and Tym chatted about the new boat to be carved from the big log washed ashore while they went in the general direction of east and south, moving up hill from riverside to the thundering gorge. "It feels good to move and shake off our long sleep." Said Cra, reaching up to a draping bud be-decked branch to snap off a tender furl of new leaves just opening. Roo smiled at her and grabbed at two more for each of them. They loved spending these stolen moments together and smiled companionably as they moved under the low sweeps of foliage and around spindly fledgling trees. Behind them, the brothers spoke in the short-handed manner of close brothers, excited to try again the adventure of the dangerous white water near the gorge and the rivers culmination at the enormous lake.

The gorge was a wild froth of river cut deep into the mountain, impossible to get over, at its centre, a violent waterfall. The Crum had found it when exploring the perimeters of the piney woods and that was when they had first met Lon. On that trip they had spent the night near his den with his permission and that was where they hoped to meet him again, though the lion's range was far reaching. They did not see him by the end of the first day when they made a shelter in a mushroom-y hollow tree trunk. It was musty and dank, but it kept them from night hunters' eyes. Nibbling on the fungus and drinking from dew-filled curls of leaves, they pulled their shums over their bodies and heads to sleep, looking so much like four large mottled coloured mushrooms.

Along the upwards travel they asked squirrels and birds if they had seen the big cat, but no one had seen him for several days. The second day they saw sign: both dried scat and huge paw prints in the occasional patch of mud. On the third day they reached the cliff of high rock and looked down at the river, so unlike to sedate waterway that it emptied into. They rested there, sharing out food and drink, sitting near the drop off, the mist rising from the gorge to curl and dampen their green hair. "We will try his den next, see if he's there." Roo told them, before extending a hand to Cra to help her up. Tym asked, "Do you think he ever made it across the gorge? He said he wanted to go over to the other side." Worried now, Roo replied, "But there was no way to cross that he knew of, unless he went high up the mountain to the river's source."

Roo lead them into the forest, away from the gorge to the rock cave with its small still pond. They walked all over the area, but no one was home. Another night was spent in the forest, this time they were secure in the lion's den, they figured they would explain when the cat showed up. In the new day Roo wanted to try going further up the gorge, saying that maybe Lon had found a way across, after all they had never been that high up the hill. They climbed the steep rocks until a jutting rock shelf made the narrowest distance from this side to the other. It was about the lengths of two trees across, the forest of pines a mirror to the wood on this side. It was where the waterfall began. There was an outcropping just below the ledge on the jagged vertical wall across the falls. When Roo scanned over the surface a movement caught his eyes: it was Lon. His dull fawn colouring blending in against the rocks. Lon was laying on a narrow shelf. He seemed to be unhurt but had no way to get up the sharp vertical wall to the top on that side. "He must have tried to jump and didn't make it." Cra was stopped in this thought when they heard an awful scream like a cat being choked. Lon stood suddenly and screeched back in frustration. "I know what this is about, the silly cat!" The brothers looked confused, but Roo just smiled.

"How can we help him?" he asked himself as well as the other three. Roo looked back towards the forest and his eye caught on a tall dead tree at the slim wedge of rock sticking out over the drop-off. It was still standing but roots looked loose in the sparse soil, one good wind would have had it toppling. It just might be enough if they could get the roots out on the forest side if they could get it to fall in just the right direction and if Lon jumped with all his might. The task was enormous, it would normally take many Crum to do such a thing and they were only four. Roo climbed to the top of the bare white branches, the tree swayed alarmingly, creaking its bare sticks in protest. On the ground again, they gathered stones and sticks and their tools, starting at the roots on the forest side, chopping and loosening them from the rock.

They worked the whole day, breaking for rests and to wave at Lon who was standing and watching them now. The tree was ready to fall over but now they needed it to go in the right direction. Cra stayed below while the three males climbed the tree. Their plan was to use their small weight to rock the tree towards Lon but climb down fast as soon as it started to topple. They coordinated the jerks and pulls on the trunk; fantastically the tree let loose with snapping roots and screeching breaks. Too fast, it fell towards the other side, the Crum descending quickly towards the rooted trunk, then had to cling helpless as it fell. Lon Leaped, the great mountain lion cleared fifteen feet to claw into the wood and scramble up the tree. The weight of the lion the last straw for the last loose roots. It was falling too fast, Lon nipped onto Roo's leg as he passed and leaped again for the rocky bank, forelegs clawing for purchase, the back legs hanging helpless. He made it up finally and spat out a bleeding Roo. Tym and Til couldn't make it, they clung to the trunk of the falling tree as it dropped over the waterfall. Cra screamed but no one heard, the water's rolling thunder taking all her sound.

Roo had a puncture wound in his thigh. Cra dressed this while Roo covered his face and moaned, horrified, and desperately grieved. Lon had disappeared into the woods with thoughts of "Water. Must drink. Water!" He came back with a dripping muzzle. "I'm sorry Roo, I could only grab one of you. Thank you for saving me, I was on that ledge for many days." His head jerked back to the gorge when the terrible screech came again. "She calls me! She's making me crazy!" He said longingly before flopping to the ground with a groan. Roo and Cra stared pointedly at the cat until he ducked his head with a shamefaced smile. "You okay, Roo? I take you home to the burrow if you want." They all moved to the gorge edge to pier over the falls. Roo sighed sadly, "We will go in the morning, it's late now and we all need to eat. They moved to the lion's den where they spent another night. Roo drank some willow bark tea that Cra made as they watched the twilight transition into a starry night. Lon went out to hunt but when they woke, he was back with them in the cat-scented den.

"They might have made it. It's just possible if the tree branches protected them and the old trunk was dry enough to float. It's possible." Said Cra as she held Roo's hand. Lon lowered his body and Cra helped Roo onto the lions back. The broad curve of back was too wide for the Crum to sit with legs spread, the best they could do was lay face down and spread flat, gripping at handfuls of fur. They made the three-day trip back in a few hours, the sleek smooth gait covering the distance amazingly fast. On the way Cra asked Lon the obvious question, "Why didn't you come down to where the river is quiet before the gorge's rapids and swim across to the other side, walk across the land until you are past the white water then swim across again? You can swim, can't you?" A jumble of thoughts came from the mountain lion, most of the words seem to be lion language swearing. "I thought of that only when I was stuck on the ledge for days. I've never tried, the water is so strong, I won't know where I could end up and don't like getting all wet! But now I wished I'd had! Your friends would still be here."

The North Burrow Crum were not surprised to see the mountain lion coming towards the burrow but wondered where Roo and the others were. When Lon came close, he laid down and now they could see just two Crum sliding off the smooth back. Blu, the gifted stone mason, was nearest and fearfully asked where the brothers were. Cra and Roo's faces told them something had gone very wrong, also Roo limped, his leg was bandaged. Cra turned to the lion and asked, "Will you stay with us awhile, Lon?" He shook his great head and turned away, "I mark around here." They watched his spraying at trunks, thankfully a distance away from them. Roo hobbled to the seating stones and when most of the Crum nearby were around them, told what had happened to Til and Tym. Pip and Dre were both away, busy working on the new log-soon-to-be-a-boat. Lis was very distraught and ran to tell the boat builders what had happened. They would want to finish it as soon as they could now. Mar had paled at hearing the tale, all colour draining from her lovely face. She at once disappeared into the burrow, with Par following. Blu suggested that they walk down to where the gorge empties into the river just in case they could see the tree caught on the rocks or even on the far shore. Mac, a middle-aged Crum and all-trades worker, said he would go with him. They would ask Fens young daughter, Exe, to let them ride on her since time was very short. All that was left still sitting were Cra, Cin, Bry and Kam.

On watch duty, Kam proceeded to climb up into the hemlock to mind the post. Roo sighed and ran fingers through his too curly hair, messy the wild locks further. "We will have our students coming very soon and must prepare for them." Cra said, "Roo, you should try to heal today. I'll take Cin and Bry to gather more food, that's mostly what needs to be done." They went inside to get the woven food baskets and then strode up the grade, picking and cutting anything edible.

Roo was left by himself at the stones. As he gazed out at the view of the river, he was a little startled to realize that it had been ages since he was by himself on this landing and had time to look at this amazing river. It was past noon, the sun a high star, the robin's egg blue vault above pierced by pine tree silhouettes on the far shore. His leg hurt, his heart worried and hoped for the brothers. He was vaguely hungry but not enough to get up and find something. Fen came and flopped down beside him like a fur-bag of bones. He gave Roo a lick on the cheek to pay him back for yelling in his ear. Roo wiped his face off with his Shum and buried his hand in the fur behind the fox's ear. He told the fox all about their fateful trip to the gorge, his students coming, maybe his parents would be bringing them as they usually did. Fen said, "I might go back with them to Home Tree." Surprised, Roo asked him why. "I'm getting too old to hunt, maybe I can get my large family to take care of me there." "I'm sorry I haven't spent much time with you lately." "That's okay, I understand." They watched the eagles from the eerie across the water as they soared and dived for the wriggling fish, trailing water streams into the air as they rose again.

Everyone that could be spared worked on carving a boat out of the large log, first cutting it apart to be the length of three raccoon bodies and as fat as Ryk had ever got. No sign of the brothers or the dead tree was found by the searchers that had gone to the gorge. Acky and his crows were asked to do a flyover to see if they could find them but no luck so far.

CHAPTER SIXTEEN

VISITORS

They had got this far when their guests arrived from Home Tree and South Burrow: A rabbit without riders but laden with full baskets mounted on its sides, a raccoon carrying Roo's sister, Lyl, and her mate, Gyn, from the south; a fox carrying his parents, Cor and Hep and walking between them, eight students, all younglings, four for Roo's training, four to be under Cra's tutelage. Cra and Roo helped Hep get off the fox (One of Fen's daughters, Weh). Hep felt stiff after the two days travel. Cor, her handsome face creased in smile lines of joy, slipped easily down the glossy red fur. While the family hugged and talked all at once, the students were welcomed by Cin an Bry, who showed them the burrow and the temporary nest beds where they would sleep. The laden baskets were taken off the rabbit, she was released but stayed close to the burrow, knowing she was protected there. The fox and raccoon climbed up the forested grade, happy to hunt in the new environment.

The seated stones had been augmented by additional carved benches from the boat log and a large table laden with a feast of freshly washed insects, salads of dressed ferns and tiny spiced fish with small tree snails. The party was lit by the golden glow of a long sunset, reflected beautifully on the river.

Notes were passed from home, news related and exclaimed over. Lyl, looking like a youthful copy of their mother said, "Our Burrow was so crowded now with younglings that some of the original older Crum have moved back to Home Tree!" Gyn added, "Your brother wants you to know that he rides on the son of Phax now, that his old Lynx has gotten fat and lazy, and now won't hunt for anyone else. Three of Phax's prodigy have riders and they keep us in furs for clothing. Lyl has been producing so much leather that she is supplying Home Tree too." Lyl now ran the South Burrow leather curing shop, a trade she learned from their father.

"Gyn has made me a new workplace, like Dedas, only bigger. "Said Lyl, proudly.

Roo told them quietly of the tragedy at the gorge and how they will work hard to find the brothers as soon as the visitors are gone. "We are thinking they could have floated on the dry tree and have landed downriver. We have sent out Acky to look and will make a new boat, but I have an obligation to the student visitors, and I won't tell them about it." Hep, concerned and looking worried, said to Roo, "We can help while we are here. Gyn and I will start carving for the next few days while you are busy with them." Roo face cleared of worry a little. "That's a great idea! Thank you, Deda."

The twins Shum-making parents seldom could travel as their father was still the Home Tree leader and their mother occupied with teaching and producing the shums. Mar and

Par sat shoulder to shoulder, huddled over the long note on a scroll of birch bark. The news was all good, reassuring and loving, telling them that they were experimenting with the making of cloth from plant fibers like the Shums, only for shirts also. They were missed and asking, of course, when could they come back.

Bry was telling the circle of students about the mountain lion and the boat they were carving, leaving out the story of the brothers for now. This kept them attentive, interjecting comparison bits about their homes throughout the stories. When Cin noticed the youngest nodding, trying to stay awake, she led them back into the burrow for the night, telling them in the morning they would visit the bat cave and the beach. Their young, excited voices was music to Cin and Bry, their energy, a balm to their old selves.

It was into the mornings soft warm rain that the Crum spilled out from the packed Burrow. Undaunted by the gentle shower, some added to their wetting by standing in the novel waterfall near the seating stones. The sun would soon dry them, even as the morning meal was eaten, welcome rays shot through the rending clouds.

The first step with the younglings was their safety orientation: they needed to understand the dangers of this northern forest. Roo would lead them with the help of Lis on the tour that began up the hill to the bat cave, always an interesting site for visitors, as well as a danger to be avoided. They followed the route of the water fall source, up the hill past Dre's home and its patch of pretty Cali lilies now in glorious bloom. Dre wasn't there. Of course, he would avoid the students until he was ready to meet them one at a time.

Lis was bringing up the rear, keeping any of the students from wandering away. One of the smallest was also one of the most precocious: Cop: bright springy curls and long-lashed eyes the colour of spring willow leaves; he kept up a constant stream of questions while darting about to investigate or prod. Lis told herself to keep a hold of Cop's Shum while looking in the cave opening.

The Cave was still not explored; it was deemed too dangerous to try to go into with its total darkness and the colony of bats. Its opening was at the near bottom of a deep crevasse, this was a chancy climb, but Roo and Lis helped the students one at a time to climb down to its leaf crackling bottom to peek into the cave, The smell of the ammonia reek of guano flowed out but they held their breath for the quick survey of the hanging sleepers along the ceilings surface. The crevasse floor had one other story to tell, the bones of a wolf that was scattered in a jumble amongst the debris. They waited until everyone was above the surface to tell them of the lone wolf that had menaced the animal friends of these woods and how the Crum had tricked the wolf into falling into the hole. Fascinated, the students all peered down into the dark crevasse and its peeking grey skull. They left with Roo's stern warning: don't even think about returning to explore the cave. This he aimed at Cop especially who grinned back at him, reminding Roo of a young Pip, always pushing at boundaries.

It was to Dre's old cave they went to next, higher up the rocky incline, a small Crum sized opening in the long wall of rock; the very top of what the Crum saw as their territory. Inside, it was gently lit with glowing mushrooms growing in vats on the floor, a space equal to the largest burrow room. They were shown the paintings on the walls telling of Dre's tragic history. "You will meet Dre later; he can hear your thoughts like you can hear the animals so too many of you at a time is hard for him. It was Dre who taught us all to swim and that's where I'm taking you next, to the beach." Roo watered the mossy bed of the mushrooms, adding the necessary nutrients. They exited the cool dim confines to bright sun to look over the hazy carpet of grey-green pines; the view of the river a ribbon far below them. The walk down hill had its own challenges for the students, both the South Burrow and Home Tree were rooted on land that was mostly flat. Here they had to manoeuvre around smooth boulders and slippery pine needles, always at a downwards slant, catching at twiggy posts and resting against stalwart trunks.

They exited the woods further down river, at a wide curve. The open beach was a welcome change, with its dune topped with sections of chopped tree log, the largest chunk the size of the soon-to-be boat. Cra, Mar and Par were waiting for them with Pip and Bry walking from the burrow, bringing baskets of food. Shums and clothes went flying, strewn about as the hot Crum ran into the water. Mar and Par joined them in the water to guard against any going too far out in the fast under current. The party was complete when Dre brought Hep and Cor, Lyl and Gyn for the food and splashing, though Dre stayed up on top of the boat log. He could hear the snatches of happy thoughts as they walked near him and that was enough; it was good to not be alone as he had been for so long.

Before they could learn how to swim the students needed to first learn the life saving techniques and Pip chose Cop to be his test dummy, figuring that he was safer under his purview that letting the youngling loose. To his credit, Cop took this well, hammy it up for his audience as Pip pretended to squeeze water from his lungs and pound his chest if his heart had stopped. Cop stood and bowed, earning a clapping ovation.

Mar and Par demonstrated the arm strokes and kicking of a swimmer before each student was paired with a teacher in the water. Cop ran to Mar and looked adoringly at her before anyone else could get to her and Dre laughed hilariously at the scene. Bob turned up to patrol the edges of the faster current, nudging up any students that flayed and sank.

That was enough for everyone, and they trudged home to the burrow. His students would sleep well, thought Roo then added," So will I!"

The next day they divided their charges into four medical trainees under Cra and Mar, and four survival students with Roo and Par. The northern forest provided unique elements to each group, and it was a good starting point for the younglings training, an education that would become more in-depth when that got back home and apprenticed with masters of the trades.

While these groups assembled and left, Hep, Cor, Lyl and Gyn went up to the Calli Lilly shelter to find Dre. It gave them a break from the chatty students, and they enjoyed the cool pine-scented forest, so different from their home burrows. Dre waited for them at his own set of seating stones by his front door, one smooth rock for himself and a small group a few feet away for visitors. His hair now more white than green, eyes warm brown, of average size, dressed as a hunter in his simple leathers and fur. They came to him over stone and leaves, pushing through new plant sprouts and past pine trunks in high-lighted flashes of sunlight.

"Hello Lyl! You brought Gyn this time, how disappointing!" he teased, wiggled his brow at Lyl. She giggled prettily and Gyn smiled good naturedly. Dre started to bow to Hep and Cor but before he could he was hugged by them both, a lovely and rare thing for him. The older couple were both so comfortable in their minds and hearts that they felt no fear that Dre would hear any thought but the kindest. "How are you?" asked Cor once they had all seated. "I'm great, they are good to me, and I provide help in every way I can. "

He turned to Gyn and Lyl, "Tell me, how is your brother and South Burrow?" Lyl answered, "Jmy and Myn and their son, Bim, are fine. The biggest change is that nine of our elders have moved back to Home Tree to make room for the growing younglings." Gyn added, "There was several coyotes that came up from the south, they had to be chased away by Phax and his sons. We lost many rabbit friends and several raccoons to them."

Dre nodded, "I've seen a coyotes, I know about them. The news here is we lost Ryk this winter, we might never learn what happened to him, but a big dead tree has landed on our beach, so Pip has a diversion. The other thing is the brothers, Til and Tym, they must have told you how they fell into the gorge. Roo is grieved and blames himself. We will find them and this time I'll go on the boat to help." Gyn told him about helping to carve the boat while the students were busy, and Dre agreed that he would join in the project. "Now! How are you doing, Cor?" He smiled and turned to Cor with an enquiring brow lifted. Cor smiled happily, something that she did much more often now that she was free from the burden of leadership. "I am fine, Dre; we rode on Weh to come here; she is the den matriarch now and rules her brood of foxes well. If I want to continue to hunt, I will have to ask one of her kits if they will allow me to ride on them." Hep draped a well-muscled arm over her his mate's shoulder, saying, "I'm glad she is around more, now. At first, I hardly saw her once she started going out to hunt on her fox." He complained mildly, smiling to show he understood her impulses. They were quiet for a while, enjoying the birds' assorted songs and the music from the stream that rippled alongside the shelter to eventually become the waterfall at the burrow landing. The ferocious scolding chatter of squirrels made them look up at the far tree. They could glimpse Weh as she hunted, her reddish coat suddenly bright as she crossed under a sunbeam. "Pip tells me that squirrels are great cursers, I'm sorry that I can't hear that." Dre smiled at his friends. "If you are ready, let's go down to the beach and look at the soon-to-be boat." As they walked downhill Hep regaled Dre with the most amusing things he had ever heard from animals. Soon the denizens of the trees heard Crum laughter sparkle through the wood.

Hep and Cor, Lyl and Gyn would go back tomorrow, taking the rabbit and fox, Weh home to the big Burrow where Lyl and her mate would wait to take the South Burrow students back home. Cor hoped that it would be Roo who brought the younglings home, it would be good to see him back at the old burrow again.

CHAPTER SEVENTEEN

THE TRAINING BEGINS

"What is this plant?" asked Cra of the tall gangly female called Bet. Cra could see that she would grow into a handsome adult but for now she was shy and awkward with her changing body. When Bet answered correctly Cra turned the question to the next student, a sharp minded male named Lir. "If you combined it with this mushroom, what would it cure?" Mar and Cra had been quizzing their group as they moved through the forest, gaging their abilities and knowledge. "All cures can be found in our surroundings, just some of them are not yet known to us, so you should always search and discover and share what you have found. Now, who will tell me about this toad stool and what it will do?" Mar and Cra taught them especially the items only found in this piney northern forest, their home burrow healers will teach them what was unique to their areas. What Cra enjoyed as well was the things her students taught her in turn, especially the South Burrow Crum with their swamp and cattails. This exchange was wonderful for Mar, also, not only did she get her training refreshed but she missed her

Home Tree sometimes and these younglings brought titbits to enjoy with their musings. At midday they were back at the burrow, they would stay at the seating stones making medical pouches of their very own. It was a personal chore that every healer must do, just has the stocking of tools and cures that go into the bags is something these students will work on all the while they were here and indeed, the rest of their careers.

Roo had taken his group to the Great Falls for a field trip that included climbing the escarpment and reviewing the territory that had once been ruled by an amazing bear. He figured that he would combine his teaching with the long overdue inspection of the place that was so close to their woods. Before they left, they were taught the making of their own spears, with Par and Pip along to add to the knowledge imparted but more importantly, to help keep the students safe, especially young Cop. They were to spend a few days with this survival training, finding shelter and eating what they could along the way. Fortunately, it was full on spring now with lots of fresh growth. The Crum from South Burrow and Home Tree were here to learn the ways of this different environment.

After a slow start of making sure everyone had back packs and tools, the all-day trek to the falls commenced with Roo leading, Par keeping Cop close in the centre and Pip at the rear, watching the amusing looks of the young Crum at Par's elbow. The three other students, two females from South Burrow, Arb and Bre and a strong serious male from Home Tree called Tip, dispersed in the middle of the group. Another reason for the slow travel was Roo stopping often to do some storytelling and teaching, with all three adults pointing out what was edible and poisonous, dangerous, or useful.

Tich joined them at the creek head where it met the river, showing off his ability to swat fish out of the water onto the bank and then splash at the Crum, making them scatter and yell. Par told him to at least throw them some little fry to lunch on. Before long everyone was splashing at the bob cat and cooling off, then drying on the sunbaked stones where the creek and the river met. That night they made a shelter next to the leaning tree, under a full bush of flat leaves and petal shredding blossoms. The great falls roared close, presenting a sparkling light show in the fading light. They would have already climbed the tree up the escarpment, but Roo and Pip could see that their handy and reliable leaning tree trunk was now barren of leaves, dry and rickety. It would be better to look at it in the full morning light. Without this mode, another route to the top would have to be found and that had too many unknowns for a simple field outing with students in tow.

Pip volunteered to try the climb first. They had their foraged breakfast that morning by the waterfall, watching the swifts dip and catch the sun sparkling droplets from the pearly curtain. It looked to be a clear and warm day and Roo was grateful for it as the tree climb would be even more dangerous with bad weather. Testing each hand and foot hold, using the extending branches and grooves in the bark, Pip went up the tree until its very top, just short of the ledge. Last time they had tried this there was some flowing grape vines that had dropped over, making for a good climbing net. It was still there though most of the vines were dry and brittle.

Pip took the greenest and tugged to see it would take his weight. As he had climbed the onlookers paid close attention to where Pip had set his weight, he was the heaviest of the group, they would follow his lead. All Crum are good climbers from their earliest years, but this tree was not very stable. Pip disappeared above only to reappear dropping over thicker stronger vines. Par went next but stopped halfway up to guide the younglings through the climb.

Roo took up the rear, ready to catch anyone falling but it all went well, and they were soon standing at the top, overlooking the rock-strewn river as it disappeared over the cliff. From this upper plain the river flowed peacefully, parted around many rocks, the larger boulders lumped along its banks. Roo gathered his students around him. "You are in a new environment, look around you for potential dangers and where you can go to be safe. Don't forget that the threat can come from above you. Both Pip and I have been grabbed by eagles in the past, thinking we were something to eat."

Roo led them along the river, looking for the tree bridge that had always taken across from side to side- and it wasn't there. It dawned on both Roo and Pip simultaneously that the driftwood log that they were making into a boat had started out up here, it must have broken loose and gone over the falls during the winter. "I think this must be the year of the traveling logs." mused Pip.

Par said, "That means hopping! I'll go first!", proceeding to leap nimbly from mossy rock to rock across the water, only once windmilling to catch her balance before safely getting to the other side. Roo called to her, annoyed for once, "Geeess!

Wait until we tie some safety lines to the younglings, I'm not seeing anyone go over anymore falls!" Roo stopped Cop before he could follow her. Par looked a little shamefaced at that but shrugged and hopped back to take across one end of several ropes that Roo and Pip tied together. In this way they all crossed safely using the ropes as a guide, at least until Bre slipped and got half-dunked. She was quickly grabbed up by Roo, earning himself his own adoring fan.

    This side of the river the forest became mixed with bright birches against the deep green of scotch pines with the pretty tamarisk and bushy hemlocks to add to the colour variety. It was mid-day and they searched out the local occupants around the near forest for conversation and direction. Roo was a great believer in working with the animal friends and often tried to ask them for help. He led them towards an old raccoon den that they had used for shelter before but instructed the students to search for the night's sanctuary just in case the den was occupied. They could stay up in tree branches if they had to, but it was far more comfortable in a cozy hole in the ground. Coming closer to it they could smell the new resident, a skunk. Young and alone, it popped it's head out of the opening saying, "Visitors! I like company!" a cheerful grin wreathing its black face. The Crum backed away laughing, Par saying, "We used to overnight in your home when coming to this place, but we will look elsewhere." This was muffled by the Shum covering her face. The skunk looked so sad that they decided to sleep in a near tree with thick low branches upwind of the den. Roo asked Seb, as he called himself, how it was here now that the bear was gone. Seb had taken possession of the den when he tried to befriend a possum family that lived there but the mother propped her babies onto her back and left, hissing. "There are only some muskrats and the flying squirrel clan that talk to me now. They told me about the Crum and that's how I wasn't surprised to understand you. The wolves patrol this area now an occasionally mark the trees here.

They were fascinated to talk to the fragrant rodent, never being inclined to speak with one before and after a while the scent became easier. It was only after going away from him then coming back to the smell that they were struck anew. They learned that the skunk's diet was like their own, mostly grubs, small fish and greens. Seb showed them his favourite food, a woven plait of river grass just under the slow current, perfect for nibbling on. It was delicious and not something found anywhere else near any of the burrows.

At dawn they were pushed out of the trees by the noisy cacophony of millions of birds greeting the sunrise. After a quick wash and meal by the river, they moved towards the aspen grove. Roo and Pip wanted to visit the bones of the great bear and check if any other large predator had moved into the wood. The great skull and a scatter of bones sat in the sunny patch, glowing white in a sudden ray through the shimmering leaves. Roo told the story of Dub, their friend and protector when they had first come to the north forest. Out of respect they left these bones alone, but bears were rare, and they could use the tools that could be made from its clean bones, so they went in search of the other bear that had killed Dub. Its remains were just outside the aspens, under a scrubby juniper. They took the teeth and claws for tools. Roo was a little surprised at the wide placement of the bones. When Seb wandered close, spreading his miasma of stink, he told them: "The wolves did that, they hated that bear. That's what the squirrels told me." They all looked east into the piney woods sloping down to finally mirror the woods across the river from the North Burrow. They knew the pack ruled that forest. Roo said to Pip, "I don't think I need to take the students farther than this into that direction, even if you did get along with the wolves before."

"Yes. And I might have to come this way through their lands in my search for the brothers." Pip pushed his straight hair away from his brow. The day had warmed and there was a moist weight to the air, clouds bunching low over the treetops. "Feels like rain is coming." said Par, coming towards them with the younglings. The back packs were heavy with bear parts and useful stones. "Why don't we take them back down to Tich's territory to complete the training and the making of spears. These packs are going to be awkward going down that leaning tree as it is." "Good thought, we can lower the packs separately and there are more shelters there that we can show them." Said Roo.

On the way back to the river, Cop peppered them with questions. Roo could see that he had a quick mind, observant and curious. Cop slipped on a smooth rock going over the water, Roo catching his shum before he could go over the falls. This led him to speculate the survivability of these falls- (after he calmed down) that they were less treacherous than the gorge, but the river was deep, fast, and wide. He sent a wish that the brothers were safe, moored on a distant shore.

"Is this what you call being on guard? Par poked Tich in his belly, the big cat was sprawled like a fur pelt in the sun in at the creeks edge.

"I was aware of your approach and deemed you as harmless as chipmunks." The bobcat stood and arched his back then yawned hugely. He looked over the wide-eyed students with his gold flecked eyes narrowed to slits in the slanting light.

Bre was emboldened to say, "Chipmunks with sharp sticks!" to which Tich grinned toothily showing sharp sticks of his own. Bre backed up and fell on his rear, eyes wide as berries.

" Stop scaring the younglings." Par scolded, then asking: "Where is the better bob cat?" She smiled cheekily while helping up Bre.

"Chi is still hunting, I think. "

Roo ordered, "Students, we are spending the night in this area. Search for a safe place!" and his charges scattered like ants. Par and Pip trailed after the students while Roo stayed behind with Tich. "Anything new here?" he asked him.

"Nothing except that Chi is breeding." Tich radiated with pride. Roo congratulated him. "We left a rope dangling from the escarpment wall, the leaning tree is very rickety now, we might have to find another route up. Any chance that you'd swim across if we needed you to?"

"I'd hate it, but I could, crossing only at the quieter, wide section, I'm afraid the current would be too strong for me. There is also the wolf pack to consider."

"That's good to know, and I hope I never need to ask."

The Crum spent the night in a hollow sycamore tree that had long ago been hit by lightning and made meals of the mushrooms, snails, and water reeds from the creek. That evening, sitting on grass tussocks, they watched the play of the setting sun sparkle on the creeks rippling surface. Roo and Pip sat companionably together and talked of the coming tasks: to finish the new boat from the log and to weave a rope ladder for replacing the leaning tree as the access up the escarpment." I hope you find them, Pip. When the students go back to Home Tree this time, I will go for a visit. Fen wants to go back to stay." They watched the students chase lightning bugs until it was time to climb into the burnt-out tree. They curled on beds of moss that they had dropped into the hollow and watched the stars through the open ceiling.

CHAPTER EIGHTEEN

THE BROTHERS

Til had jerked his weight over to the other side of the gorge in tandem with Tym and Roo and felt the snapping roots loosen and the dead tree tilt. No time to get down! Suddenly it went over, and they all clung to the trunk and branches. Lon leaped, claws extended and just missing impaling Tym on his mad scrambling leaps up the falling tree. They tried to follow the lion up the trunk, but the roots released just as the mountain lion leaped for the ledge, Roo clasp in his mouth. It was all they could do to hold on while the tree fell, the branches cutting troughs in the veil of waterfall. The world was all motion and fear until the crash at the bottom, rocks smashing and snapping the branches that thankfully spared the Crum from hitting bare rock. Then they were under the brutal tumbling waves, clinging with all their strength and holding what breath they had. Tym was knocked by a rock and lost his air, opened his mouth to water. Til grabbed at his arm just as he let loose his grip and held his brother until the trunk bobbed to the surface. The tree was hurtled down the gorge, tossing to and fro, once turning upside down only to slap into the immersed rocks at the gorge's violent exit into the river. Til pulled Tyms limp form onto the top half of their tree that bobbed above the surface. He pounded on his back, hoping to expel the swallowed water, hoping to find a place to use the lifesaving actions, hoping to keep them both on top of the ungainly raft.

Finally, Tym coughed and threw up water and groaned. His brother was relieved and couldn't stop holding Tym even has he raised his head to see where they were.

Sweeping down river, its remaining tree limbs scrapping at hidden rocks and jerking their transport about. This slowed their transit a little until they came to the long curve of the river and the large pile of wood debris piled on its bank. They were on the same side as the burrow, but the impassable gorge lay between them and home.

The tree snagged into the dead fall of wood just long enough for the brothers to climb off and onto the largest piece of driftwood. Then their tree screeched apart from the bank to continue its voyage down the river. Wanting dry land and a surface that didn't rock they carefully weaved and climbed through deadfall wood until finally on land, a thickly wooded forest of pines just like North Burrows. Crawling to the nearest fir, they sat against the base to take stock of the injuries and bruises. Tym coughed and rubbed at his sore chest, Til was cut along his face but not deeply. Both were badly bruised, stiff, and cold. Delayed reaction set them shivering though the day was still warm. After a while, Tym croaked, "I must be alive, I'm hungry!" said Tym. Til smiled then tears filled his eyes, and he couldn't reply, just patted his brothers leather clad knee and nodded. Soon he got up and searched for food- grubs as always were easy to dig up and with a few of the spring fern shoots that broke through the leaf strewn forest floor. After eating they would find the rivers edge that was more assessable and have a drink.

Like the North Burrow wood, the land here steeply sloped towards the river with sudden boulders and crevasses amongst the fragrant pines. Birds and scolding squirrels, darting chipmunks, and scurrying mice, all avoided the strange grey creatures and didn't heed any of their calls. "We need to find a crow that will pass the news on to the other Crum, they will be looking for us and worrying."

"How are we going to get home?" Til asked himself, knowing the answer was," Not without help" as they would need to cross the river again. That meant finding someone to carry them across. Somebody big. Back tracking to the gorge they searched for help before the water churned too much and made it impossible to cross. The crashing noise and mist filled the air, and all the surfaces were wet. Shuddering in remembrance of their near fatal miss, Til said: "I wonder where the female mountain lion is that Lon was after, she would be big enough to carry us across." They got the answer from a squirrel who stilled enough to answer them from his perch on a damp and mushroom-y stump. "Gone, and we are so happy! No one could sleep with all that calling to the other lion. She has gone back up the mountain where she lives, who knows when she will come down here again." He twitched once and ran into the underbrush.

They were missed by the searching Crum and crows, the full foliage obscuring the small, camouflaged Crum.

That night was spent in hole in an old fallen log. The small hollow was a bit spidery, but the web caught and held the smaller bugs on one end, and they lined its floor with large clean leaves. Their shums were still damp but they curled close to each other and slept fitfully, with Tym coughing sporadically.

They were awakened by a loud knocking on their log. Groaning with sore muscles, Tym swatted away the curious spider as big as his head before immerging out of the hole, scaring away the red-headed woodpecker before he could ask about any other animals here.

The morning was thankfully still sunny and clear. They began the journey down the river, moving along its bank. It was the same way they had travelled that summer on the boat that ended up at the mouth of a huge lake. They hoped to not have to go that far, to cross as soon as possible as they still had to pass through the wolf packs territory on the other side, up the escarpment, to cross the river at its milder upper region then down to the Burrow. They needed animal help!

CHAPTER NINETEEN

STUDENT TRAINING IS OVER

The medical students were assembled at the burrows circle of seating stones with Cra and Mar demonstrating the bandaging the reluctant patient, Bob. There was nothing wrong with the otter but as he was loitering near the burrow waiting for Pip to come back and Mar had pleaded so sweetly that Bob found himself prodded and wrapped while being fed nibbles of food.

This was how Roo and his group found them when they arrived home from the excursion above the great falls. Pip roared with laughter at Bob who snatched off his head bandages and scooted into the river at the sudden influx of laughing Crum crowding the Burrows landing.

Roo hugged and nose-bumped his mate as she smiled and told him he stank like a skunk. He grinned and hugged her more until she pushed him away towards the waterfall. "I'm glad you are back. Now go wash!" He was joined by the whole group, showering with a paste of soap berries, and scrubbing down their clothing while the meal was brought out and fresh shums and clothes pulled from the students sleeping nests.

The bear parts were examined, and Pip told everyone of the visit with the helpful Seb. In turn, Cra sadly told that there was no news about Til and Tym but that the boat construction was far along. As soon as the visitors were gone the boat finishing would commence in earnest.

The younglings would be going home in two days with Roo and the twins traveling with them. The filling of the large woven baskets that the animals carried would start the next morning. Salt, pine nuts, snails and mushrooms were plentiful in the north woods and the hunters would take back many raw pelts for Hep to cure once back in his workshop.

Tich was spoiled, he hadn't carried baskets for a long time. One heavy basket on each side of his body, with straps going across his back and chest and another under his belly. "You've gotten chubby. At least you won't have riders as well as the baskets." Mar tucked smooth cushioning under the strapping while Par held the bobcat's cheek tufts, daring him to stay still a little longer.

Roo was checking back packs and counting heads, He caught Cop's Shum just as the Crum tried to hop down to the river. "It's like herding a bunch of mice!" he thought.

The flash of pale russet caught his eye. It was Fen coming towards the Crum gathering at the landing. "Fen! It's good to see you up and around, ready for a fun trip?" Roo looked at his old hunting partner. He was showing his age in his white muzzle and bony thinness, but his sepia eyes shone with energy. "Tich is taking the baskets, do you want a rider or two occasionally?" asked Roo.

"Sure, I can be at the back of the students and catch any who are tired or stray."

That was how the assembly set off, with Tich leading, the twins setting the pace with him, the students walking in the middle and Roo and Fen at the rear, waving goodbye to the North Burrow. The morning was cloudy and warm, it felt like rain was coming. The trip there should take two walking days, first west and south, following the riverbank to where the rocks split the waters flow into the creek, then south down the creek's path until the Home Tree: an ancient and giant oak growing close on its banks. Under its wide girth was the largest Burrow where over one hundred Crum dwelled.

For Roo and Fen, it was a wonderful return to the days when they were carefree hunters, before North Burrow and Roo's responsibilities.

Fen nosed Cop back with the others while Roo passed out food packets of leaf wrapped fruit and nuts. They had made the first stop at the head of the creek after a quick detour to the Great falls so the medical students could see it again. As always, its majestic power amazed, even on a cloudy day.

After the rest they continued south until twilight when the animals were released to hunt, and Roo asked the young Crum to find a sheltered spot to overnight. Tich and Fen slipped away in different directions, leaving the baskets for Roo to look after. He was just looking up at the trees for possible places when a fat drop of rain splashed on his face. Fen laughed as he was coming through the pines and low spruce. He stopped being amused at Roo when a sudden deluge started in earnest, soaking them as if they'd been dunked in the creek. The fox and Crum settled under the thick low branch of a juniper that swept the ground on its heavy end. It was mostly dry there, the thick bed of rust-coloured needles made for a prickly cushion. Fen stayed tucked in with the eleven Crum, but Tich found another tree for his night. The best part was Fen's warm fur that they all pushed against, Fen mumbled that it was a lot of wet Crum. They just giggled, grateful for the tolerant fox.

Morning was a murk of dense fog. They could hear the creeks babble, but the adults kept the younglings close and moved along the bank with caution. The animals had no issue with the fog, their keen sense of smell and hearing made up for sight. By noon it was clear again, they made the final stop for food, everyone excited to be so close to the large burrow.

Mar and Par had not been home for many seasons and their parents had only visited once. Roo had been gone the longest away- it had been ten seasons. The once familiar terrain and paths seemed strange, even the smells were different. They were arriving in the late afternoon, the Watch Post Crum calling out welcome and the younglings running ahead to be greeted by the many Crum going about the place. At the great old oak tree of the burrow, Roo met his mother tending to the barks lichen, removing pests and debris. She smiled with joy then quickly called into the open entrance, letting the inside know of their visitors. Roo swung her around in a wide hug. Suddenly it was crowded with greetings and students, parents and Tich and Fen asking to please remove these baskets and all the other Crum come to the exciting noise. Bip and Ryh enveloped their twins, remarking on the changes in them and telling everyone of the feast planned in the common room. Bip chuckled at Par's braid and adorning feathers. Their daughters were beautiful and amazing.

Fen disappeared as soon as he could to the old den where his daughter and the extensive warren lived along the well-travelled path to the south. Tich bounded away north, the hunting here was poor and, he'd have to go far to find enough food, way away from this protected Crum land.

Walking through the ancient tunnels lined with carved and polished wood softly lit with niches of clustered phosphorescent mushrooms, the smell immediately taking him back to being a youngling here. Everything seemed worn and smaller than he remembered. He would spend his nights in an unfamiliar room, Hep and Cor had moved into this small back room when Jmy, Roo and Lyl had gone on to the north and south. The only thing that was the same was the smell of Hep's leather working corner, bringing dreams of the youth of Fen, the freedom of hunting and exploring without a care. Jmy and Myn had returned to South Burrow, but Lyl and Gyn had stayed to take the students back to South Burrow. The family room was crowded, and they spent much of their time outside or in the common room. His sister would leave the next morning, so the family talked well into the night in the larger common room about their burrows, both so different, the environments each having unique challenges. They were often joined by other Crum, leaving notes and imparting news. Roo and the twins were popular and exciting. The younglings found them brave and novel, the old thought they were daring and reckless but not without a with a small jot of envy.

Earlier, Roo had a difficult visit with Ute, the remaining parent of Til and Tym, explaining the fall into the gorge and the belief that they had survived, how they were carving another boat to find them. She was an older, female version of the brothers, with a strong short stature and practical nature. Though shocked and worried, she was realistic- that finding them was far from easy or certain. She thanked Roo and wished him well; the weight of guilt and worry was only too evident on Roo's face.

Fen was surrounded by fox kits and mice remains as he draped on the dusty hard-packed dirt, the sun shimmering on the white hairs in his red coat.

"I've come to say goodbye, Fen, I'm going back north tomorrow." Roo had enjoyed the walk to the den through the forest of maples and oaks, the flat land refreshing after years of walking on sloping ground, but now the time had come for the parting from his old friend, another of the many changes for Roo. "Mai knows I'm not coming back; it's been hard on her having all but one of our kits gone and I don't hunt so frequently." Roo hugged the fox's neck, Fen complained that he was getting him all wet with tears, then gently licking Roo's face.

Tich danced around impatiently growling; the refilled baskets bobbing at his sides while the Crum said their goodbyes to Roo and the twins. Only family had come out to see them off at this very early morn. It was going to be a very hot day, the sun very bright and the southern wind pushing at their backs like a warm hand.

Mar's lose hair whipped over her face as she followed Tich's bobbed tail, Roo and Par bringing up the rear with spears and pipes ready for use; quiet now that they were on their way. It happened midafternoon: a mole ran between Tichs legs in a desperate flight from a badger. The big carnivore slammed into the bobcat's side, knocking the basket askew. Then it was all teeth and claws and screeching until the combatants were both hurt, and the badger ran back the way he had come. It all took place so fast that the Crum couldn't do more than blow their pipes one piercing toot. Roo surveyed the damage. The baskets were torn off Tich, one was broken and the furs, clothing, shums, bottles of juices and other special liquids flung across the path and forest and floating in the creek. Tich had a bite across his nose and a clawed stab in his side. Mar took care of the cats hurts while Par and Roo waded into the water for the soaked goods and found all the scattered items. Only one basket was still usable, and the straps could be retied and cut anew. Tich would have an awkward walk home with only the weight on one side, but they would place the most perishable items in it and the remnants of basket and goods were buried and camouflaged under a nearby prickly bush. They would spend the night there as the events aftermath took up all the afternoon, and it would have the added benefit of allowing Tich to recover and Mar to keep checking for infection. They huddled close to the cat under the bush. It was warm with Tich, but they had to put up with a buzz of angry mutterings about badgers and baskets and all things that were annoying, including Crum.

Roo watched the half-moon through the silhouette of thorns and leaves as they swayed in the wind, now reduced with the evening's coolness. He dreamed of the dead tree as it swayed above the roaring water and suddenly falling, screaming then choking. Waking with a sudden shudder, he wished with all his heart that Til and Tym were safe. Mar whispered, "That must have been some dream." "Yeh, I was falling into the gorge." She replied, "I miss Til. When we find him, I'm going to become his mate." Roo looked at her determined mouth, just visible in the waning moonlight. "Does he know that?" She chuckled softly. "No, but I know he won't mind, he just thinks he has no chance with me." Roo touched her face with understanding then turned into the bobcat's warm fur to catch the remaining hours of sleep.

Par came up with the idea of unearthing the largest of the fur blankets, filling and tying it to counterbalance the weight on Tich and that was how they set off in the late morning, the delay would have them not reaching the burrow until well late in the night.

Cra watched and waited, taking the watch duty on their hemlock branch that evening. The crows had told her that they were coming' along with the report of no news of the brothers. The night breeze rocked the tree, warm and soft. Coy, the spotted owl dropped next to her and chatted fussily about the silly squirrels and a difficult snake eating all the mice. She sent her on her way with a firm wish, "Good hunting, Coy!" The bob cat was coming, his great night vision taking the Crum directly to the burrow. Roo let the others release Tich while he quickly climbed to Cra, hugging and nuzzling. She felt like home and smelled like joy. Sitting side by side on the branch, he told her about the trip with greetings from her mother and everyone and what happened with the badger. She, in turn, told him that the boat was almost done, that they still had no sightings of the lost Crum. When his eyes drooped closed, she sent him down to rest while the night continued peacefully, her heart at ease now. The avian noise preceded the dawns glow and then Bry came to replace her, he was bright eyed and happy, still strongly muscled, his head topped with waves of soft white hair. Bry thrived away from Home Tree, she thought. This made her think of the other elder here, Cin. She was slowing dramatically now. Cra would walk with her to find her burial tree soon; like all Crum her body would rest under the roots of a tree when her spirit has left it. She thought Cin would hold on until the boat crew left.

CHAPTER TWENTY

THE BOAT

It was as big as the last one, the length of two full sized raccoons with tails attached and as wide as two Ryks at his fattest. They made three benches across this time and made the bottom wider and flat for stability. Pip had cut more handholds and rigged ropes along the gunnels and a stone anchor that sat next to the boat on the sandy beach. It was a large stone that they had painstakingly bored a hole through and attached with a rope to the boat.

"We wanted to have the anchor ready in case a storm come up or something and the boat went off on its own to the river." Pip told an admiring Roo.

Bob waddled out of the water and joined the morning crowd, his head going up and down in his usual cheerfulness. "I help!" Pip scratched behind his small ear, making Bobs back half gyrate comically and the otter closed his eyes and hummed.

"We can go as soon as the supplies are laid in. Lis, Me, Dre and Blu."

"Me too." Said Mar. You might need me, and even more, Til and Tym might need my help." When Pip and Roo nodded, she added firmly, "You couldn't have stopped me this time."

Dre was coming on this trip. He had learned to ignore most of the stray thoughts coming from the other Crum and even found it handy at times, like when Pip and he were working on the carving, Dre would just hand Pip a tool without he having to ask. Dre also had experience with boats, though the small rafts the Mountain Clan had used on their lake was quite different than this big boat on this fast river. Still, he was excited, ready for at least one more adventure.

Lis had done this before. That made her both scared and determined, wanting to improve from the last trip, to stop before they river emptied into the lake, to find the lost Crum and see the wolf clan again. The pups would have grown would they remember her?

Blu knew that Roo would miss his talent with the pipes and stones and hoped that the Burrow would be fine while he was away, but Roo would not begrudge the opportunity for change. Roo thought the same way, that was why they were all here in the north instead living quietly in Home Tree. He had wanted to go the last time and was torn between settling the plumbing to the burrow and the unknown of uncontrolled boat travel.

Pip hugged his sister and then Roo. The sailors all clambered aboard while the anchor was lifted aboard, and the Crum pushed the boat the last distance into the river.

It was caught by the current. They dug deep with the oars to direct it to the centre. They had no time to look back, the flat bottom kept them steady, the fast water swept them along and out of sight of the watchers within seconds.

They steered the boat as best they could to the other side of the gorge but quickly, they were rocked by the rapid white waves, shoving off rocks that appeared, moving from side to side to keep the boat from tipping. Lis's oar was suddenly wrenched from her arms when it caught between two boulders. She braced her feet wide and held onto the gunnels. They were tossed like feathers in the wind, the boat turned about face and sideways, tilting suddenly onto its side, water rushing over the gunnels before they threw their weight to the opposite side and slammed again flat. Then they were hurdling past the gorge until the surface finally smoothed out. The forest whipped past; rows of trees bordered by undergrowth crowding the banks with no place for a landing in site. The Crum were wet and breathless, hands bruised and arms and shoulders feeling like they had been wrenched hard. From the lessons learned on the previous trip, All the supplies and back packs were still in the boat, tied securely though soaked through.

The first curve came at last, the flotsam piled there in a dangerous jumble, sharp limbs ready to catch the small craft. They were almost upended there, a long limb of a giant dead tree caught at their boat, then the weight unbalanced, and it loosened from the pile and tumbled into the water, tipping river water into the boat. Pip pushed it away using muscles grown strong from pulling fishing nets while the others bailed with the large snail shells that were hung on the gunnels. They had made it past the bend and slipped into the straight stretch that Pip had remembered. He relaxed a little and told them to start looking out for their friends, "They could have landed anywhere along here."

CHAPTER TWENTY-ONE

RYK

The mushroom was delicious, meaty, and earthy. Til chomped his half in great bites and washed it down with handfuls of cool stream water. Til was more reserved in his eating, watching the forest for animal danger or help. They had been walking for three days, slow going through the dense woods, the heated air heavy with humidity and mosquitos. They couldn't bite through a Crum skin but were very pesty, the flies couldn't resist trying to land anyway. Food had been plentiful, but they were getting tired. The nights were spent in tall trees. The plan was to stay close to the river but follow it down stream and hope to find a big enough friend to take them across to the wolf's territory, then maybe another animal willing cross the water when past the gorges violent water. Til had his watch pipe in hand as he walked, grateful that it had stayed tied to his belt through all the calamities. They both carried rough made spears though Tym used his as much as a walking stick, as a spear. The bruises had faded, and his coughing was better, and the weather had been so far, rainless, if hot.

An old raccoon was washing a small fish in the river, thin and patchy-furred. Tym gasped, "Its Ryk!" the Crum ran towards him, ducking under limbs and over rocks. Ryk turned at the voices in his head. They heard a tumult of thoughts from him, joy uppermost but also weariness. "Hello Tym, Til. You found me! I didn't think I would see another Crum again. Is Pip here too? I miss him." Ryk sat slowly on his backside, belly showing pink bare skin where skin sores bloomed, tail looking hlf the thickness it should be. He ate a little bite of fish then set it aside.

Til asked: "What happened to you? Yes, Pip is fine, very worried about you. I think he figured you were caught by a big predator over the winter."

"Not a predator, a chunk of ice. I went down to the river to wash my food, the ice I was on broke away and I was floating downstream until the gorge water. I fell in then and almost froze until I caught the wood at the rivers curve and climbed out. Again, I almost froze until I pushed deep under a leaf pile and snow fell then and I was finally able to stop shivering. It's been hard living since, I'm lucky I haven't been eaten yet. I wish Cra was here, she could fix my sores at least." He waved a paw at his blemished torso.

Ryk had made a den out of a space between two close trees, where he could run up the trunks if danger came near. With their arrival he seemed to deflate somehow, to no longer want to move from his nest of old fur clumps and leaves. They took care of him as best they could, bringing him food and talking to him. Til told him how they had come to be here and that they were looking for someone to take them across the water, to find their way home. Ryk sighed, I wish that could have been me." Then one morning the raccoon was still and cold.

"I wish we could have done more for him." Said Tym sadly. "At least we can tell Pip what happened to him... when we ever get home." Til handed him his walking spear. "Let's go and find a way to see them again!"

A huge dark shape bullied through the tangle of black spruce, the biggest moving shape the Crum had ever seen. It had enormous, rounded horns, a long heavy droopy nose, and legs like dark tree trunks. It dipped its great head to the stream, beard trailing into the water. "What is that?!!" whispered Til.

"I think it's what you call a moose." replied Tym. The moose swung its head to peer at the Crum, its eyes surprisingly small. "What is you?" asked the moose, making them smile. "We are Crum. Is there any chance that you would swim across the river to the other side? We need to get over there." Asked Til, backing away a little when the giant head swung even closer. "You want ride? How you hear me, I hear you?"

"That's what Crum can do; we hear the animals. We want to go home and that means we need to get to the other side. You won't even feel us on you, you are so big and strong!" Til tried out some flattery.

The moose named Bul shrugged and allowed the Crum to climb a near tree then jump onto his back then scramble up to the fuzzy horns. Tucked behind the fat curves they felt slightly protected from branches as the moose moved through the forest, unfortunately in the wrong direction. 'Bul seems to have forgotten us already." thought Til, breaking a leavy branch to use as a fan. The moose had his own personal cloud of black flies. At first, they were so grateful to be getting a ride that they let him wander, zigzagging from edible to edible. "Bul, where are we going? Can we go to the river to cross?" said Tym, getting worried.

"I go where I want. I eat everything. I sleep when tired." And proceeded to nod off, standing.

"Bul! We want to cross the river!" The moose slowly bent his knees and dropped to the ground, snoring loudly. The Crum climbed down to the ground. "Now what do we do?" Frustrated they decided to stay with the moose just in case they could make him go back to the river. They tucked in close to the brown shoulder. "Just hope he doesn't roll in his sleep and squish us." Said Tym

Bul woke with a shaking snort, his big nose bitten and swarming with insects. Til and Tym had just enough time to grab on to the course neck mane as the moose hauled himself up and began crashing into the brush, away from the river, the two Crum stuck to his fur like two clingy seed pods. No amount of calling did any good. Bul kept chanting, "Bugs on nose! River has bugs! Bad bugs on nose!" They were lucky not to be on the antlers as Bul kept shaking his head and pushing into leaves to remove the pests, but they suffered a battering from the same bushes until Til yelled, "This won't do! Grab the next branch!" and that was what they did. Clinging like draping moss to the green branch they could see the moose rump disappeared into the brush. The thin limb bent low with their combined weight, and they dropped to the ground.

Til straightened his Shum and lamented, "We need to eat and then get back on course. I wonder if he will even notice that we are gone.?"

They sighed and began the trek back to the river, searching for their dropped spears and any food along the way. It took them all day until finally they were gazing at the smooth reflected sunset and its distant shore. They found an empty ground nest that smelled of old minks and were grateful to sleep on the ground again, once they had chocked heavy sticks across the opening.

It was the next afternoon that they were distracted by the clamorous sky battle between three crows and a hawk. Til and Tym had been high in a tree, trying to see how far they were to the water and if any animals big enough to swim its current were in view. They saw the trio of crows and were about to call out and wave when the hawk had flown down from the blinding sun to attack the first crow, killing it instantly. The other two set up a huge cry of woe and danger that made the Crum the forget for a minute to look to their own safety. They were being stalked. The marten, a voracious member of the weasel family, had never seen a Crum before and had climbed silently up to a limb just behind the trunk. Claws extended and sharp teeth ready to rend, it leaped at the two brothers. The blur of motion out of the corner of Tils eye and he pushed his brother off the branch and dove after him, the marten snapping at Tils Shum and catching just the end of it as he fell. Til choked, the Shum catching his neck and almost breaking it before he twisted and it slipped off him, allowing the Crum to free fall after his brother. Tym fall was arrested with the stomach smack unto a lower limb that knocked the wind out of him then he slid off again to land on a full spread of leaves spread like an open hand to catch every bit of sun. He caught onto them, and his fall was stopped, and he looked up to see his brother falling right on top of him and then the two Crum hit the ground, softened only by a thick pad of old loamy leaves. The marten was leaping from the tree right after them, determined to get his meal of whatever they were. No escape! No breath would come and dizzy from the hard hits, it was all they could do to curl up tight into balls. Tym had the Pipe, no time to use it. It opened his jaw as wide as it could and bit at Til, the top fang stabbing into his shoulder but could not get a grip with the bottom jaw, the tightly rolled Crum was just too big. An awful taste flooded the marten's mouth and it gagged and grimaced and spit and gave up. By then Tym blew the pipe and the marten had enough and ran up the forest slope.

    The wound was thin and deep, and Til was in in paint. They packed moss into the hole and found a place to recover on the ground in a short hollow between roots. It looked like the beginnings of a Crum burrow, and they took it as a good sign. Til had a sore and bruised neck and Tym was black across his stomach. That night Til was feverish, and they wished again for Cra or Mar to help them. Til spoke of Mar especially and sometimes seemed to see her in the tight burrow with them. They spent three days there until Til was recovered enough to move his arm and the wound seemed to close. Tym had climbed up to get the Shum out of the tree as it was caught on the leaves, sticky with sap.

Their luck turned the next day when they met the beaver family. Signs of gnawed bark and downed trees, clean white wood shavings bright against the dirt and leaves foretold of the activity of beavers. They followed the sound of a dragging limb until they came to a glossy brown creature with a paddle shaped tail and impressively long yellow front incisors. Coming along side of the beaver, Til and Tym said hello, making the beaver pause. "You are funny looking squirrels," it stated, then continued its mission. They walked with it, weaving away now and again to avoid the stabbing points of topless trunks. Til started the now familiar explanation but was interrupted with: "If you must talk (though I don't know how!) you must keep up! I am very busy." It was headed for a stream that fed into the river. A sizable obstruction was already backing up the flow of water, eating into the forest on either side. The two Crum dove into the clearwater with joyful abandonment, drinking and laughing and making such an odd spectacle that the beavers stopped the construction to watched them. Out from under the pile of stacked wood dam popped two more beavers. The largest smoothly arrowed her bullet shaped head straight for the Crum that now sat on a rock near the water's edge. With small brown eyes blinking, she asked: "Who and what are you? Why are you in our pond?" They stood and bowed low to her, perceiving that she was a respected matriarch of the colony. This time Til tried for deference: "We have been on a long and terrible journey. It's wonderful to be awash in fresh cool water. We are sorry if we disturbed your pond."

The first beaver told her, they say they are Crum, whatever that is."

The large female huffed, and they both slipped into the water, getting back to the work of tucking, and twining the branches into the pile while to two Crum foraged for food and dried in the sun rays coming through the canopy. At sunset they slowed, chewed the small wood and the first beaver came and sat by them. "I am Sat. Where is your home?" "We live in a burrow, one that a wolverine had made. Its past the gorge, halfway to the great falls. Do you know where that is?" As Til spoke the brown eyes grew wide with respect. "That is very far! I've never gone so far although my cousins are on the other side of the river, trying to make a dam home there.

"I've seen them! A few years ago, we made a boat - floating wood- that took us into the big lake. We had to cross into the wolf's forest to get to the top of the escarpment. The river is easy to cross up there. We need to get across this river as soon as we can, it will be a long trek still to go home."

"You have wandered far for things that are so small. Us beavers can swim to the other side, though we usually do it underwater. The current is strong, and we end up farther along than we started but we can do it. What if you hold on to some wood that I carry in my mouth. You will get dunked a lot. Could you hold on well enough? I need to ask my mother, maybe my sister can take one of you, too."

Tym almost cried, "Yes! We can make a rope that we can tie on just in case we fall in the river!" They ran to the downed green stalks and began stripping the stringy sinews to twine into ropes, Til doing what he could with his stronger arm.

The morning saw two sticks with ropes attached on either side and enough in the middle to tie up a desperate little Crum. Sat knocked them awake. "Hurry! We have work to do. My sister-cub will take one of you." They explained the ropes and sticks to the beavers and soon were sitting along the back of each one, holding on to the ropes as it passed each small ear and tied around each Crum. Before they could say goodbye, they were in the water, holding on for dear life as the currents pull tried to push them off the beavers' backs. Then they were underwater, bouncing has the beaver undulated though the current, then rising and taking a breath then down again until they could hardly stand it. Clearing the surface, Til let lose the sore arm and lost one handhold and was flopping against the brown fur when Sat pulled him onto the muddy bank. Sat laughed at the grey Crum now a uniform green- mud coloured with only the white grins and sparkling light brown eyes different. The beaver, now free from Crum and ropes, called, "Good travels little Crum!" and disappeared into the water.

This forest looked much like the other side that they just had come from. They weren't sure where they were in relation to the gorge or the wolf pack's den but still it was a major step. With lighter hearts they moved into the woods. They would follow the river back upstream on this side until finally they could start up the steep climb to the level of the escarpment.

They couldn't know that as soon as they moved into cover of the brush that the small wood boat was passing by; that the searchers, sleepy from a long night on the water, had just flowed past and not seen them.

CHAPTER TWENTY-TWO

BACK ON THE BOAT

"What if we don't see them at all? We could have missed them!" Lis said what they all had said and thought and there was no answer, they had to try. The plan was to stop the boat before it reached the big lake by dropping the anchor and steering to the wolf side. Secretly, Pip thought that this plan was optimistic, that they were small Crum on a big fast river, Lis was the only one who might understand as she had taken this boat ride with him last time. Now it was pleasant. They had tried to stay awake through the night but the hard day before and the smooth ride had lulled them into dosing. Blu had passed out food packets and jugs of juice. The sun grew stronger, the cloud of flies attracted to the juice smell pestered them. Time and again they started at a movement along the shore to find that it was the forest animals coming down to drink. A family of beavers, a moose! (The first any of them had ever seen) and dipping birds of every size. They were joined by a small gaggle of geese that came to float alongside, curious at the strange log and its occupants. When one had pecked at the boat, they were so distracted that the river suddenly widened, and they flowed into the very lake they had sworn to avoid! Dre threw out the anchor and every oar was dug deep into the water to push the boat to the shore. The boat was dragged along the lakeside until the anchor caught on something unseen and they twirled in the eddies, close enough to swim ashore. "Quick, before it's let loose!" yelled Pip and slung his pack over his shoulder and dropped into the water, they all copied his lead. It was a short way to shore but the sodden packs made them struggle and sink until with the strongest swimmers helping the slower, they crawled onto the sand like drowned rats. From the sandy beach they watched the boat as its anchor rope broke and it float serenely into the vast centre.

"We keep this up and we'll have abandoned boats all over the shores of this lake." Pip ruefully mumbled. Of course, everything in their packs was wet. The food was quickly eaten, the shums and clothes hung out on bushes to dry, and five naked Crum laid on the beach to dry like sun basking lizards. Lis sat with Mar, brooding over the futility of the mission, she had so hoped to find them before reaching the lake again. "Our old boat was about half days walk up that-a-way." She pointed to the side of the lake. Mar said, "Of course it will take the help of animals. They know what goes on in their territories. We need to ask everyone, especially the wolves."

Pip roused everyone to redress and pack up the still damp items.

Although they were technically in the same woods as the brothers now, they were many miles apart. Pip's group was well north at the lake and Til and Tym scrambled alongside the river west and south. The brothers wouldn't mind meeting the wolf pack again but kept moving along the river, trying to avoid getting lost in the interior wood. They inquired often to many of the animals that they met along the way, just as Pip's bunch did, "where were the wolves? And in the case of Pips group, "Have you seen creatures like us?"

The large rock outcropping that the wolves lived by was generally in the woods centre. Both Lis and Pip remembered well the time by the pond and cave of the pack.

At that time two of the young canine had given them a swift ride to the edge of their territory, cutting the travel time through the forest and their trip home enormously.

After two days of many fruitless directions given by mischievous squirrels and chipmunks who sent them in many directions, they found it, and to their chagrin, it was deserted. Dre, Blu and Mar had never been to a wolf den and took the opportunity to inspect the rocky and canine smelling cave and detritus of the packs home. That night they spent in the den, secure at least in the knowledge that no other animal would dare to invade the place. Blu sighed and flopped by the pond. The air was oppressive, even when they bathed, they would hardly dry in the high humidity. Mar and Lis joined him, passing out scavenged grubs and some tender new leaves. There was a strong smell laying over the whole area, made worse by the heavy moist air, the wolf-y musk that overwhelmed the usual woodsy fragrance.

It was Dre that first became aware of the lowering lead-coloured sky and the silence in the forest. The wind had arrived and was pushing at the small Crum. Sending leaves and branches into flight. Their hair suddenly lifted away from their scalps, charged with a life of its own. Dre yelled, "Everyone get into the den!" Blu, Mar and Lis hopped over rock and tussocks, fuelled by Dre's panic, they just made it, but Pip was the farthest away. Suddenly Pip was blinded and thrown into the air, thrust away from the lightning destroyed tree. A deafening explosive clap of thunder made the ground tremble. The wind, a giant hand, wiped across the forest. Mar's eyes refocused after the blast of light to see Pip, awkward and motionless against a pine. A solid curtain of rain slanted in a solid sheet, obscuring all sight from outside the den. Mar felt beaten down has she struggled into the deluge, then fell to her knees to crawl in the direction that Pip was last seen. She was afraid that he would drown. The thunder growled and lightning flashed continually, the rain seemed to bounce from the ground and pool, making her movements slippery with mud and slick grass. She felt around ahead of herself as she crawled, blinded at times by the flashes, until she felt his leg. Pip groaned. Mar moved to be near his head, pulling it from the growing the puddle, now madly alive with hard splashing drops. "Can you crawl? "She yelled. Mar helped him to his knees and together they began the crawling return to the den's shelter. Hail, the size of pine nuts stopped the progress and made them curl into balls with their hands over their heads. Dre, Blu and Lis looked out in horror and worry, helpless until the hail stopped. As suddenly as it had come, the damaging hail ceased, and the rain lessened enough that the others came to help them into the dark cave. Pip lay in the dimly lit opening so they could see the damage done to him. Most of his straight hair was gone, a weird green frizz was all that was left. His right boot was missing, the sole of the foot, red and blistered. Pip twitched and shuddered. He grimaced and drew a shaking hand over his bare head.

From Blu: "What hurts?"

From Lis: "How do you feel?"

From Mar: "How bad is your foot?"

Dre told them, "Give him a minute, he's not thinking straight yet."

It took several minutes until Pip eyes refocused, and he was aware of them all staring with worried care. He croaked, "Ahhh! "My head hurts! And the pain goes all through my leg!" Mar brought him sips of water from one of their leather pouches that used to hold juice.

They made him as comfortable as they could, watching over him through the night as the rain fell steadily though not as heavy, the wind continued but not as strong.

Til and Tym burrowed into the wolf's belly fur while the storm raged and crashed around them, the old wolf trembling and flattening her body as much as she could trying to disappear into the ground.

They had found the pack the day before as they were hunting. Twenty-three wolves were moving silently through the undergrowth. It was only when the two Crum called out to them that the leader stopped at the familiar voices in her head. "You Crum have come back!" She started with surprise, finding the almost invisible creatures a short way away, blending into a clump of grass.

"It wasn't on purpose this time. We fell into the gorge and floated down the river on a tree!" Til told her. It was just interesting enough to make the pack stop and listen. When they finished their story, one of the young males asked, "Are you trying to go up to the falls again? The bear is gone now."

"We know! Yes, we need to get home. Do you mind if we travel through your land? Tym asked politely.

The large female leader lifted a bony shoulder in a shrug. "We must go that way to get back at our place by the rocks and pond, our den. You can come with us." The pale coloured young male came up to them, grinning. "I'm still wondering if you taste good!"

"Oh, you were the one who wanted to chew on us. Now you've all grown up and so handsome, too." Another wolf passed, tsking, "Flattery! He thinks he's handsome enough already!"

The Crum walked quickly, trying to keep up with them until a kind elder named Syl allowed them onto her back. They thanked her so profusely that she threatened to dump them off her if they didn't keep quiet. They heard her but could sense her goodness and reached up to scratch behind her ears. Moving through the trees, one or another wolf would occasionally dart after small prey. The Crum tried to ignore the crunch of bones and small cries of pain. Everyone had to eat.

The storm starting with stealthy whips of wind and gusts of cold rain that alarmingly increased in intensity. The wind became a furious gale. At first the wolves continued, heads lowered, slung low and battling the push of strong wind like giant hands trying to knock them off their feet. Thick wet fur smell filled the faces as the Crum clung limpid-like on Syl's back.

At the first crash of thunder, surprised yelps were followed by the pack running flat out until the hail had them stopping and flattening their long bodies to the ground with ears laid back and eyes white-walled, to lie under every low tree and bush they could find. Gale winds swept the branches of trees sideways and toppling not a few. Syl made no protest when Til and Tym squished close to her side. They could hear her thoughts of: "Ow! Too loud! Wet!" and "Stop now!". Worse was the lightning, each violent flash followed by roaring thunder. The ground shook as much as the trembling wolf. They suffered through hail beating them, bouncing off the animals and accumulating around the Crum. Branches broke and flew, the crash of tree damage adding the tumult. Finally, the rain eased to a heavy but more normal summer shower, the wind was not as brutal, and Syl said, "We go now." She shook mightily and lowered herself for the Crum to get on her back again. Now the surface was filled with pooled water, the brush and grass clumps poking out like islands, everything reflected on the surfaces. Through the all-encompassing grey, the Crum took no note of the direction, grateful not to be walking in this and knowing this land had become unrecognizable anyway.

The storm hit the North Burrow tree with vengeance, swaying and shaking the old hemlock, making the glow of the mushrooms on the Crum faces shift and move. Although they had created what they thought was sufficient channels to pass the accumulation of rain harmlessly through the burrow, the tunnels had become so clogged with much more debris that they were soon overwhelmed. The lower levels of the burrow began to fill with water. Bry and Par did their best to unclog the stone waterways and Roo and Mac were outside shoving leaves and branches out of the channels until Cra dragged them back inside before they too were washed or blown into the raging river. The hail began, bonking hollowly on the tree trunk and forcing all the Crum waited it out in the protection of the large main room. They could only listen as the crashing storm made the very walls shake and the hemlock groan. The ground heaved and dirt filtered between now splitting wall panels; they feared the whole tree would be ripped out from above them. There was a rumbling shake, and something smashed into their burrow tree. Its walls trembled and rocked, and Roo was suddenly sure that the tree would uproot and fall into the river below. Would they be pulled into the raging torrent, helplessly caught in the roots all around them? How was Pip and the others? Did they find a place to be safe in this crazy storm? Were they whipping around on the big lake, helpless has a leaf? Roo thought of the other big storm: when his father was hurt by the dropping limb of the Home Tree Oak, the size of a grown tree. This storm was worse. Many Crum had died that day, and his father was never quite the same after the damage.

A chipmunk was trembling next to the Crum, it had dashed in just as they closed the burrow door. Cra had her arm wrapped around the shaking rodent, mummering calming words. Roo noted a small pile of fresh fragrant pellets under its tail and mentally sympathized with its feelings. When he sat on the other side of Cra on her bench, she shared the fur blanket that she had grabbed from their bed and covered both her and him, lending her small warmth through his wet shum and leathers.

Bry checked on the slow rise of water filling the lower levels and thought with despair, "No one was getting to sleep tonight anyway." The burrow had had three levels. Most of the daily living was done on this top floor, only sleeping rooms were below. Now even this large space felt unsafe and hollow. Bry thought of Cin; they had laid her body under the young spruce she had chosen only a few days ago. He was the eldest here, now. "But I've never seen a storm like this in all my one-hundred and seventy-three seasons!"

Mac and Kam had commandeered the Make-Well bed and its blankets to get warm and Par joined them to add her heat, filling the nest to overflowing.

The weather settled finally to a steady leaf-filled wind and simple but constant rain. Relieved the burrow tree was still standing, Roo opened the entrance door and stepped out to the landing. He could see the cause of the hit the hemlock had taken: a big pine had pulled out of the sodden ground, its roots naked and exposed, the needled crown fell to the river, sweeping the surface of the rushing water. It had hit the hemlock with its outer limbs, the heavy trunk just missing their home tree. Near the landing the usually gentle waterfall was huge, cutting its own gorge into the high riverbank, pushing out rocks and mud from above made loose from the cavernous new hole of the fallen tree. "Oh, no!" Roo cried. "This whole landing is about to be washed away!" He set everyone to work at making barriers to the water flow away from the burrow while Par fought through the sloppy mud and pushing rain to the fox den crying for help. The two foxes braved the wet to help with repairs, carrying rocks in their mouths twice the size that a Crum could carry. Running next to the home of the raccoons, Par asked again for help and then found the otter to join in the work. Bob came to the burrow by the river, fighting the strong rushing current until he could use the fallen pine to get out on land.

At sunrise the exhausted Crum and animals had managed to create a big enough wall of rocks to shore up the bank and corral the heavy flow of downhill water. They sat on the ground, every seating stone in use or gone. Drops from the tree's leaves were the only rain falling now, everyone had mud from head to toe. Grim and bone-weary. Roo hung his head, arms propped on bent knees.

Cra said what they all were thinking: "I'm sorry, Roo, but we need to find another burrow. This was too close; our tree won't survive this, certainly not another storm."

Bry sadly added, "We are only six Crum here, the work to get this burrow habitable again is more than I can even think about right now."

CHAPTER TWENTY-THREE
THE MEETING

Pip had slept well, waking in the morning with a headache and a sore foot but was able to hobble about with Lis's help. They were deciding what to do next when the wolves appeared out of the morning fog, ghostly silent, making hardly a splash in the diminishing puddles. Pip, Mar, Lis, Blu and Dre hurriedly vacated the domain of the predators and moved over to a close tree with a large, raised root that made a perfect bench.

Suddenly Mar cried out with joy: she had seen the passengers riding on the back of the older wolf. Tym and Til were waving madly. Syl, relieved, flopped down to let her friends slide off her back. The Crum ran to each other, all but Pip, who sat with a sheen of tears in his eyes. The wolf pack ignored the Crum, tired after the storm. They lay on the stones like damp rugs while the Crum all talked at once, telling of the travels and astonished how close they had been to each other at times. It was amazing to be together at last! The brothers told Pip of meeting Ryk and his passing. Pip nodded and thanked them, glad to know at last what had taken his friend. After a respectful pause the two lost Crum both said at the same time, "Let's go home now!"

Blu had made a walking stick for Pip. Not only was his foot burned, but he also no longer had a boot. They wrapped and tied the foot with any spare leather the others had.

Til went to the matriarch of the pack as she lay just inside the cave. He asked if any of the wolves would be willing to take them closer to the escarpment. She didn't answer quickly, and the Crum hung close by, quiet and enjoying the relief of the mission accomplished, of finding the lost brothers. They couldn't help but touch and sit close together, so wonderful was the joy and amazement at their luck.

At the end of the day, they were approached by the three puppies they had met on the last trip here, now grown. They would take them at least part of the way to the escarpment. "Now? asked Pip.

"We like the night. Moon tonight. We can hunt on the way back." said the largest male. He would take Pip, Dre and Lis. His brother allowed Blu and Tym to climb on his back and the smaller sister took Til and Mar.

Moon rays shot through the tree canopy, touching all the surfaces with degrees of ghostly blue and white, making it possible for both Crum and wolves to see the passage through the tall trunks and brush. The group finally allowed themselves to relax and enjoy the smooth gait of a canine, though the wide back required all the Crum to sit very spread-legged.

It was a magical evening, especially for Mar and Til. Finally, she could hold him close as she rode behind Til, breathing in his warm masculine scent and feeling a fierce need to covet this moment, this future. For Til, it was as if all his dreams were coming true, he was breathless and tingled from head to toe. Mar had made it clear that she cared about him in the special way that only mated Crum had for each other; mating for life, plus he was going back to the burrow with his brother and friends and- not having to walk all the way! The small wolf that moved beneath the couple heard little conversation but had noted with chagrin that it felt like one Crum riding, not two.

Moving amongst the trees they witnessed the storms wrath, seeing quite a few trees uprooted and lying on the ground. Pip suddenly had a terrible worry: how well had their burrow fared through this bad storm? They had left so few Crum back there, could they handle whatever this wild weather had wrought?

They were let off in a clearing, well into the dead of night. With much thanks to the three wolves, they watched them blend away into the shadows, then look for somewhere to shelter. Awkwardly Pip followed the others up a huge oak where they would secure themselves in its wide crooks for the rest of the night.

The morning came. Back on the surface, a mixture of crushed leaves, fugus and mud was spread evenly over Pips burned foot, immediately soothing and easing the pain. "Huh! That's great, thank you Mar!" Once the limb was rewrapped, Pip found he could walk easily. The route was obvious, even without the directions given by their canine transport, they needed to go up. The land began a sloping climb from the pine and oak tree forest they had landed in.

Pip had come this way before, with Roo on the back of the bear, Dub. Everything looked different now, and the storm had dropped trees and limbs and left huge puddles, and of course all the animals were new to him. They stopped often to climb under and over blockages of wood, speaking occasionally to the animals that would stop to chat. A family of raccoons were friendly but busy with digging a new den after theirs had collapsed. A large flock of bandy-legged turkeys quickly passed, necks thrusting while unaware of an intense and silent lynx that winked at the Crum and continued after them. A colony of hares were curious but went along in their great hops after a few hellos. Two days had passed, and they had wandered further north than Pip had travelled on his previous trip.

It was in the large maple grove that they saw it: An amazing giant tree, a maple old and strong alongside of a large ground-fed pond, the smooth surface perfectly reflecting the huge tree. It had high raised roots stretching wide over the land until digging deeply into the soil. Its trunk was knobby with burls and moss, the crown as wide as a cloud. "It's bigger than Home Tree, I think!" said Blu, awed by the sight. They all came and laid their cheeks against the bark to listen to the sap-song. Pip checked out the burrows going under the tree roots. They didn't go far, just enough for small groups of animals to house there. Pip looked long at this place and wondered at the possibilities.

Reluctantly, they left the tree with its gentle pond. They continued up the slope, now steeper, weaving on deer trails up to the level of the escarpment. Finally, they reached the aspen grove, a recognizable place to stop and spend the night near the huge skull of the bear. Being so close to the burrow lit their hearts, just one-half day's walk to the escarpment and down the leaning tree, and another half days trek and they would be home. The shushing of aspen leaves played over the weary Crum as they huddled into the crooks of the branches, too excited to sleep.

The morning breeze carried the perfume of the skunk to them. Til and Mar woke to the scent from a branch in the tall white tree and watched the black and white stripes cross under them. They waited until the skunk passed away from them before climbing down. When Seb came to Pip's tree Pip landed in front of the skunk and laughed as the skunk jumped then affectionately bumped into Pip. He pushed him away with a smile. "Good morning! How are you, Seb?" The rodent happily went from tree to tree to greet the descending Crum who distanced themselves as best they could and pulled their Shum's over their faces. Seb must have sprayed recently, the smell was freshly pungent, enough to make their eyes water.

"I am happy! You stay? Where is young Crums?"

"They went back to their home burrows. Sorry Seb, we want to go to North Burrow as soon as we can. Til and Tym have been missing a long time and we must get back to the home."

"I go with you. We eat food together." Pip led the way to the river while telling the young skunk of the adventures, including the wonderful maple tree and its pond. The others trailed a respectable distance behind, fearful that Seb would get startled at something while they were close to the gently waving tail. Mice and squirrels scattered in their wake while the birds chuckled and tittered in their safe heights seeming to be laughing at the skunk escort.

Large rocks were strewn on the riverbanks and dotted throughout the riverbed the water faster and higher than before.

The waters flow bubbled and parted around the rocks and painted the sides with green algae and foam.

"I miss the tree bridge." Said Pip as he carefully hopped from rock to rock while Seb swam, keeping pace and chatting non-stop. The rest of the Crum followed with various degrees of grace, with Til and Tym telling themselves, "Don't fall! And Careful! It won't do to go over another waterfall!"

They moved the short distance to the grape vine that dropped over the ledge and found the rope they had left there had been chewed away. Lis went over the side first while holding on to the strongest vine that draped over the cliff. They heard her exclaim: "It's gone!" and she scrambled back up. They took turns to lay on their stomachs and peer over the edge at the broken tree trunk far below, the top half dipping into the waterfall's foam.

Tym sat back in a weary funk. His brother draped and arm around his shoulders. Pip gave a sigh and faced his friends. They were all filthy and exhausted, tattered, and hungry. "Okay, we must find another way down, and on this side of the river. Let's eat some food here by the river." Seb was the only one who was cheerful that his friends were still with him and happily gouged scars into the earth to expose the fresh grubs and from the river he knocked water snails towards the Crum. They all felt better for the meal and a good wash. Even Dre grew easy with the skunk after a while when his behaviour showed him to be harmless. They had gotten used to the smell… mostly.

Discussion ensued over the situation: "The old leaning tree was going to fall sooner or later, it's too bad no-one got around to placing a good rope ladder that extended all the way down." said Pip

"It might have gotten chewed up too." Claimed Til.

"What if we follow along the escarpment wall on this side. Sooner or later, it must slope down just like it did on the way into the wolf's land." Said Blu.

Dre added, "If we need to get back to the great maple tree, we need to find a way that your animals can travel to it, carrying all your goods." They all looked at him in surprise. "You must see the tree as a possible future home, it's much like my Mountain Burrow with its small lake. Trees don't live forever."

"Yes," answered Pip, "It's wonderful, but would Roo leave his North Burrow? And It's even farther away from the Home Tree." After a pause he roused them up to start the exploration of the edge of the escarpment, moving southwest now. They followed the land, keeping a small distance from the drop off and looking for places where the slope was easier. They found several where they could have made the dangerous descent, but they were also looking for a place that made the ascent doable for animals and Crum. Seb went with them, strolling behind like a rear guard. When asked what he was doing he answered that he was curious about what they would find, he hoped they didn't mind.

The forest was bright with a mix of full leafed maples and oaks with a medley of pines and spruces. They found the same mix of animals here too as the woods across the river: chattering music from the treetops, scurrying and scolding from the surface. A herd of twenty or more deer shied away from their calls, long slim legs springing weightlessly away. A bad-tempered badger sprang at them from under an aromatic bay leaf bush and chased them away from his territory. They caught their breath at the top of a hill of flowering grass that seemed to be at the end of the badger's range. From its rounded top they could see the gradual slope, the march of trunks gently undulating but still slanting down. In the woods again, they strode through the waves of sun and shadow into the afternoons dusk. Gratefully they found a large, downed tree, hollowed out with time and big enough for all the Crum. Seb was kind enough to seek his own nest after Mar explained that they only had room for the Crum, Behind Seb she could see Til making a face and rolling his eyes. It was all she could do to keep a serious face until the disappointed skunk turned away.

Before they curled into their Shum's to sleep, Tym told them about the spiderwebbed log they had slept in on the first night, how he'd awaken to the large spider exploring his face. He paused and added seriously: "I haven't said thank you for coming to find us. You put yourselves in great danger without knowing if we were even still alive."

"Had to try." Choked out Pip. "Not knowing is hard to except."

The bright light of dawn shone right into their log. They had lived so long in the dim evergreen woods that the direct unhampered rays coming over the short grasses required some adjustment and shading of their eyes. They saw Seb marching back and forth in indecision. "What is wrong? Pip asked him. "I want to stay with you, but I'm scared of your woods." wailed the skunk.

"We can't help you decide but it might help to know that it's possible that we will eventually be coming to stay at the big maple and pond and leave our North Burrow. You have choices, to come with us now, to go back to your den above the falls or to start a new home near the maple."

The small black eyes blinked at them, and he grinned a black-lipped smile and nodded. "I go find the maple. I make new home. Maybe...find another of my kind!" Decision made he turned and ran away, back the way they had come.

They moved eastwards into the woods until finally they met the familiar creek that they called Home Creek. Following it south would take them to Home Tree, north to where the creek was born from the big river, then east again downriver until they were back! Suddenly it was all familiar and comforting, they knew these trees and rocks and critters.

The first moments of unease came with noticing the many of the familiar trees were down and there were a lot of broken branches. Tich did not meet them when they came abreast of his den. At sunset they were in sight of the burrow woods and could hear a flurry of activity, chopping wood and animal growls. The Watch Post was unmanned; indeed, the tree was chocked at an awkward angle. Everyone was too busy to notice the rag-tag travellers until they stood in shock looking at the fallen massive pine pushing against the burrow hemlock, the deep holes and diverted waterfall. Par yelled in surprised joy at the site of them and everyone stopped working including the two foxes, two bobcats, and an otter. Roo saw the two brothers and burst into astonished tears. Til and Tym ran to him and comforted him saying, "It's alright Roo!" Cra hugged the three of them and then everyone was there in a super hug, even Dre, with Bob yipping and bobbing next to them and the other animals looking on.

Pip and Blu surveyed the damage and work done so far with Roo tiredly pointing out what he thought needed to be done next. Roo was relieved to have his best friend and such strong workers back, he had despaired at the daunting task of getting the Burrow liveable again. They all had been sleeping crowdedly in Dre's cave, Dre's old shelter was damaged and needed work, too. So far, they had cleaned the second lower floor and did a rudimentary repair to the plumbing flow to the burrow.

Pip let him talk until Roo stopped with a tired sigh, then Pip spoke of what Blu and he were thinking: "We found a wonderful tree that could be a perfect burrow though it will take a lot of work. Roo, its big enough to be a long-term home, even bigger than Home Tree, with a small lake that we think is ground fed next to it!" Cra joined them as Pip was talking and gasped, "Roo, this could be an answer. Pip, where is this tree?" Roo stopped any reply with, "Wait, let us get everyone, I want to hear everything, and this is a decision for all of us."

The animals had been working under Par and Til's direction, attempting to shift the downed pine with little success. "It's going to take several bears to move this" muttered Tich, tired and sore and wanting to leave this mess to the Crum. When the halt was called, he flopped down to listen next to his visibly pregnant mate.

Pip told the seated group around him of the giant maple tree with its large pond. "It's far from here, west, northwest. It will take Crum walking four or five days. We found it after the wolves dropped us outside their territory, more north than you and I, Roo, had gone with Dub that time. It's a forest of mixed trees mostly maples, like Home Tree woods, with mostly level ground, with a good harem of rabbits and many other animals though we didn't see any top predators other than a lynx nearby."

Dre said: "The tree has large roots as tall as we are that extend out from the trunk a long way. A few burrows have been made by smaller animals some ways under the tree; we don't know how far."

From Mar: "I think there is at least one owl living in the high branches, the whole place has a healthy crop of animals if you go by the many tracks made as they came to drink at the pond."

Blu added: "I would need to discover the spring that feeds the pond and divert some of the water to the tree but from the surface it looks possible."

Roo looked at Cra to gauge her reaction to this and found her smiling and radiant. As dirty as her face was, she never looked more beautiful to him. He asked the group at large, "What do you think? Who wants to stay here, who wants to go back to Home Tree and who wants to make a new burrow under the maple tree?"

Dre spoke first, "I will go to the new tree, but I'll need to make a separate shelter nearby. I think this group is ready to grow into a proper burrow." He carefully averted his face from Cra's, least his face show knowledge of what she was desiring.

Many voices spoke all at once, all the Crum were wanting to try this move. Only two animals would not join them. Chi said that she would stay and raise her kits by the creek, Tich should go away now". No one was surprised at this; male bobcats did not stay around after the birth of the kits. The two foxes we ready for the change, it wasn't the same here without Fen; plus, the Crum would need them for the transport of the baskets.

Bob was sad. He couldn't make the long trip overland; his world was this river. "I will be alright; I'll go along the river and look for more otters."

CHAPTER TWENTY-FOUR

THE EXODUS

Roo took one last look around at the North Burrow. The pine was pushing against the hemlock, it was only a matter of time before it would knock loose the upper roots and they both would be in the river. He felt a weird mix of sadness and excitement. Pip stood beside him, gazing at the river that gave him so many trials and enjoyment. The pond will seem tame in comparison. Bob had gone days ago while they were busy packing up their belongings and gathering food from these pinewoods. He and Roo were the last Crum. They turned as one to follow the two laden foxes and one grumbling bobcat and the walking Crum. Only one rode on a fox, Bry, though he had stated that he would get down to walk occasionally.

Acky had never come to them. Finally, another crow brought the news that Acky was killed by a hawk and the rest of the crows had lost interest and stopped looking for the missing Crum. Roo relayed to the new crow what his group was doing, and could he please give this news to the Home Tree Watch Crum. Also, if they could keep a watch for the Crum's progress to the new tree so they knew where to bring news.

Roo thanked Waq, the new crow, enthusiastically, glad to have the Home Tree Burrow know where they could be found.

That evening they stopped to enjoy the big waterfall, spending the first night listening to its rumbling rush. Chi came to say goodbye and good luck and they thanked her and wished her joy with the new kits. While the others were making a comfortable nest, Pip went to sit in the dark by the water before he would join them to sleep under the usual tree. He was saying good by to this great water, and maybe to this part of his life. When Cra came and sat near him, he swiped his face dry and said, "Pretty isn't it?" And it was, the moonlight made the drops glow like millions of tiny lights, the swirling rush a deep indigo and soft violet. She said nothing, content to let the river talk. Eventually Pip sighed, "You and Roo will be happy in a bigger burrow."

Cra had thought about it and replied, "I will be but maybe not Roo. Here he was living wild and teaching and nothing was boring. I truly hope that he will find enough purpose at the new burrow."

Pip stood and helped her to her feet. "One thing is for certain; he's going to be occupied digging for quite a while!"

The next night was spent near the prairie grasses. Tich and the foxes, once released from their baskets, could be seen hopping through the long stems and leaves to catch and gobble the many mice that usually lived peacefully there. Many of the poor rodents streaked past the Crum as they sat in the hollow log, while Mar told the story of Seb the skunk who had left them there many days ago. It hadn't rained but kept cool and cloudy all day, something that was welcome when they were forced into the direct sun while navigating through the grass even at the forest edge.

Morning presented them with a steady soft rain to accompany the travellers as they moved up the slopping ground, going through dampened leaves on the ground and making and hardly a sound. The light coloured everything a soft grey as it neared twilight and they looked for a place to sleep. The Crum could stay in the trees but where could they store the baskets? In the end it was decided to stay on the ground with the foxes and their burdens, huddled between two rocks. Tich patrolled and hunted during the night after the foxes had done a short trip of hunting before settling down with the Crum. They were near the grassy hill where the badger lived and had no wish to try to discover his area limits in the dark.

The smell of a skunk came on the breeze in the new daylight. Mar speculated that it might be Seb but that he was staying away because of the bobcat and foxes. "Til and I should walk aways ahead of you so Seb will be comfortable enough to approach. If it's not Seb, that will be interesting, too!"

When the two Crum were a long way into the forest and the smell had grown stronger, they heard a quiet hello from a bush of trembling leaves. "Seb, is that you?" asked Mar. Til added, "Don't be afraid of the animals with us, they won't hurt you if they know we are friends." They backed up as Seb came out of his cover. "I so happy to see you! I wait and wait. I want to show you a good way to the tree. You will be away from mean old badger and it's a shorter path than coming along the cliff edge."

"That is great, Seb! You can wait here; we will bring the others and you can lead us all on the new route." Til and Mar retraced their steps and soon the caravan of cat, foxes and Crum followed the wafting scent of the skunk across the woods in a slightly wandering line to the aspen grove.

"That cut out some travel time." Said Pip. The Crum were comfortably settled for the night in a bridging arch of rocks. They had made a steady progress north, skirting the aspens and moving into land that was never seen by Crum. This rock bridge was part huge pile that looked like a giant had dropped out of a bucket into a rough mound. Under the arch were seasons of old soft leaves that made for a good nest. The one side was enclosed by the foxes and the baskets the other. "Tomorrow we should be at the maple grove." Dre said. Roo sighed, "I'm excited to see this wonderful tree but also, I'm not looking forward to the hard work of making a new burrow. As soon as we can we need to get word back to the other burrows, we need help, and many might want to stay, too."

They arrived at the edge of the Maple grove at late afternoon of the following day.

The amazing Maple was mirrored in the pond that was big enough to be called a small lake. Slightly oval and surrounded by reeds on one side and rocks falling down the gradual bank on the side closest to the giant tree. They all marvelled at the size and glory of them both. From the side that they had arrived at, it would take half a day circle the pond and reach the tree. That allowed the Crum to observe all the animals that came to drink and lived all around this grove. Tich could hardly be restrained from chasing the wild turkeys, but Par told him he only had a small way to go, before he could leave off the baskets for good. Roo was figuring how would they ever control the multitude of animals that would have to come daily to drink here.

The girth of the trunk was awe inspiring, lumpy with burls and sprouting a light coat of small mosses and ferns; it was beautiful to the Crum. As one, the Crum left off their packs to touch the tree's bark, ask permission to alter and occupy, to live in its harmony. Feeling no negative vibes and only peaceful acquiescence, they set about asking the foxes to clear out the small rodents that were housed in the several burrows going under the trunk roots. That was where the Crum would start to excavate a large home.

They wouldn't cut roots but gently redirected them, clear openings of the dirt to gradually make rooms. Once the walls of the space had settled, they would enclose the walls with fresh curving wood planks, some of which had arched holes cut into them for the phosphorescent mushrooms to be planted. It would take many seasons before the new burrow was much more than a woody cave, but they would work hard to have it ready before winter.

Word of the venture had travelled to Home and South Burrows through the crows; Crum came from the two other burrows to help get it liveable. This meant increased food gathering and the making of friends with all the surrounding animals. One of the first things needed: Roo and Pip had to climb to the top of the Maple as soon as they could to see the full area and meet the great horned owl that lived in its hole in the trunk. It was a long climb up the trunk and a long time before the lowest limbs curved off the trunk.

Roo moved onto a lower branch that slanted to face the owls nest hole. He called hello and waited for the great horned head to poke out, golden eyes as big as a Crum's head. "It is about time you've come to see me! This is my tree that you are making holes in!" Roo bowed low while clutching at the leafy branch. "I am Roo, and this is Pip. We are Crum." Pip waved from a still lower branch. It really was a long way down. "We won't hurt this tree but nourish it and are careful not to cut any of the roots. I hope that our coming won't bother you. Crum only want to live in harmony with the forest and the animals."

"Humm. I'm called Haws. I've never spoken to a tailless squirrel. Are you tasty as a squirrel? He thrust his huge head out towards Roo. The leaves trembled that Roo held on to. "We are not squirrels!" The owl tittered then let out a huge squawking laugh. "I was checking your bravery, little Crum. I suppose that your being here makes no difference to me. Plenty of food to find here. You must tell me about Crum. Where are you from, how is it that we understand each other?" With the threat averted, Roo sat comfortably on the branch and told the bird all about their journey, the Crum and what will probably happen to this place now that the Crum will live here. "My mate, Cra and her helper Mar are healers. They will help heal the hurts of the animals that need it. The Crum will have Watch posts on the surrounding trees to warn away any disruptive predators though we will allow them to drink. But we protect the smaller animals in our territory."

Pip had been looking around below at all the activity of Crum and animals, everything looking tiny from so far up. A series of screeches and growls drew the attention of the whole area's creatures, all came to a stop to watch the inevitable cat fight taking place on the far side of the pond. Tich had confronted the Lynx. Both were in their top form, full adults, and the same size. Roo sighed and the giant bird maneuverer out to stand on Roo's branch and watch the show. "The bobcat is Tich, he came with us from the north forest." Roo told him. The owl said, "That's Kap. He's okay; hunts mostly north." Just then several Crum blew their pipes with their piercing sound that made the owl wince and most of the creatures run away into the forest. "That is very effective!" said the owl in admiration. The two combatants had drawn apart, still snarling. Par was seen approaching them, palms out to each cat. They couldn't hear her speak but eventually both cats moved into the woods in opposite directions.

Pip said. "I'm happy to have met you. I'll go down now. Blu needs help with the stone pipes." Roo was quiet as his friend descended. "It's nice and peaceful up here." Perceptively the owl noted that the Crum was delaying going back down to the work in the burrow. "Come up anytime. I've enjoyed this new experience, talking to you strange squirrels." Tittering, he then launched into the air, almost unseating Roo.

"They agreed to hunt in separate areas and keep out of each other's way." Par told Roo has they stood near the new entrance door. Crum were going in and out of the big opening, its door braced open to the side.

"Was Tich hurt? Was Kap injured?"

"Oh, that's his name. Not too bad, but it will take some talking to make him comfortable enough to let Mar treat the wounds. Tich has added to his scars; nothing serious."

"The owl up in our tree is called Haws. I like him." Par looked at the quiet expression on Roo's face. "You miss Fen. Maybe you could be an owl rider like your sister?" Smiling at the pretty hunter, he answered, "Maybe. But not today. Today I'm laying stones in the floor below!" He made a false excited face wiggling his brow, making her laugh before he headed inside and down the new tunnel to the lower level.

When Pip wasn't helping Blu with the stone pipes that went from the pond to the burrow, he walked through the trees around these new woods. He didn't know what he wanted; he just missed the movement of water. For as long as he could remember, he played and fished in the Home Creek and then as an adult, he fished in the river. What was he to do with this pond? He could scoop the small fish there in nets but too much of that would reduce the stock of minnows. Ryk was gone, too. He could make friends with a new animal, maybe. He wasn't a hunter like Roo or Par. He was trying to see how he would fit in at this new place.

Dre helped the burrow and himself by staying out of it. He set up a wood carving area in the most logical place: where a very big tree had fallen, probably in that same storm that did so much damage that summer, not too far from the burrow. Gyn had come from South Burrow with five other Crum and he and Dre were busy making nest beds. Lyl had sent with him many fine fur pelts for the new beds. They needed to make all the round and oval concave shapes that would sit on short platforms from this tree. It looked like the new burrow would be home to fifty or more Crum, has many of the younger help wanted to stay once the winter had set in. Dre had found a good shelter for himself close to his work. It was another animal burrow under an oak, recently vacated. He quickly took it over, first making a good door, then shoring up the walls with fresh panels. It had smelled faintly of raccoon but with the fresh wood, glowing mushrooms and stocks of edibles, the small burrow soon felt like a home. Gyn had accepted Dre's invitation to bring in one of the newly made nest beds and stay with him instead of the crowded burrow. There was plenty of room and they got along well.

At the backside of the maple tree, one of the small animal nests holes had been expanded into a large Make-well room with tunnels to the big burrow rooms. One of the first nest beds made were the special raised ones needed for the healers and a large table for the treatment of hurt animals and Crum, though most of the animal care took place outside near the doorway. This was Cra's and Mar's place of work though they spent the first few days meeting with the various forest denizens who came to drink. They told them of the work that they do, that they could come to get healing help. As soon as they could, they went in search of the medicinal fungi and leaves a make-well needed, then set up the various containers for the herbs and potions that they had collected from the woods. It was an extremely busy time! One of the students from the summer had come back to stay and learn from them, Bet. When not dealing with animals, they had many Crum with cuts and bruises from the hard work of setting stones and cutting wood.

Til came into the Make Well with a large shelf he wanted to mount on the wall above the bed. Mar set aside the tying of leaf bunches to nose-bump her mate. They would have the mating ceremony in a few days. He still couldn't believe his good fortune, that this amazing, beautiful creature would choose him. For Mar she saw his kind, warm eyes, strong shoulders, and good heart. He had no idea how special he was. The brother's mother had come to help and maybe to stay. Almost losing her sons was the reason she had come but this wonderful place had her thinking of staying. Ute liked Mar and had known the twins all their lives, and she loved working again on new wood with her sons.

The two foxes, Mai and Exe were surprisingly well accepted into the established fox den. The oldest female had just past, some of the wilder males had left already and the two healthy females were just what the troop needed. Mai encouraged the other foxes to accept Crum riders.

Seb was so very happy! Not only did he have many friends with all the Crum, but he had also found another skunk, a female that seemed to enjoy his sharing of her home. Even the big pond had its small fish and frogs and many delicious insects.

CHARTER TWENTY-FIVE
THE CEREMONY

Roo had his arm around Cra while they looked on the joyous couple standing near the pond. All the Crum had stopped work to watch the two say their vows. It was just before sunset, a glorious day of perfect temperatures and small wispy clouds. Mar had a new leather set of clothes decorated with tiny leaves and flowers. She wore no Shum. At this ceremony her new mate would encompass them both in a special large Shum made for two, upon the saying of the vows. From Home Tree had come Bip and Ryh, bearing the new shums, they stood with Ute behind the couple. Mar's face glowed as she placed a circle of leaves around Tils neck and said the same common Crum vows that Roo and Cra had joyfully said: "Will you be mine? I promise to protect and care and provide. You are my forever." Til gulped and tearfully said: I will be yours. I promise to protect and care and provide. You are my forever!" He placed the extra-large Shum he wore over her head and body. Their hug was interrupted by everyone butting in with congratulations and cheers. Mar and Til replaced the big Shum with new individual ones, signalling the start of the party. Even Tich, sitting a short way away, was happy for the Crum though he thought the ceremony totally unnecessary.

On the flat plain between the burrow door and the pond was a large new stone table where food of all kinds was brought out of the burrow and set there. The table had become the eating place for when the weather was good. When it was too windy or wet, the largest burrow room had many smaller tables and comfortable seating that all the Crum shared.

Roo watched with affectionate observation and a raised brow at the changes in his friends as they sat and stood around the table. Tym sat at Tils elbow to tease and toast the new couple. Many former students laughed together as they boasted about the merits of their home burrows. Pip sat apart with Gyn and Dre, Gyn trying to explain the nature of the swamp to the mountain clansman. Pip had been quieter since coming to this new place. Roo was worried about Pip and would talk with him soon if Pip didn't figure out what he wanted by winter.

Sparse white hair and thinning cheeks, Bry was looking very tired but happy. Par, Kam and Blu surrounded him, listening to his old hunting stories.

Many of the guests would be going soon though some would stay and be very welcome. They would have to go back before the cold weather set in, especially the South Burrow Crum, it was more than seven days walk away. Already Roo could see a few of the trees' leaves tipping with gold and russet.

He caught Cra's eyes as she spoke to her new apprentice, and they smiled at each other. She had tied her long hair up with flowers for the ceremony and the setting sun blushed her cheeks. He knew she was very happy in this new burrow, there was room here to grow, and to grow old in.

They had made him the leader of the burrow without voting and that was fine for now. He would make the watch lists, direct the construction, and ensure that the food gatherers kept the pantry full. In the spring he would figure out what he wanted also. Like Pip, he felt unsettled, too young to stay full time in the burrow and hungry to heed the call of the unknown. He missed teaching and meeting new animals in the wild environments. Soon this burrow would fill up and settle into mundane routine.

The silent passing of his new owl friend caught his eye as the soft wind ruffled his green curls from his brow. He was smote anew with the beauty of this place, this moment and was grateful.

The End

www.ingramcontent.com/pod-product-compliance
Lightning Source LLC
LaVergne TN
LVHW010202070526
838199LV00062B/4467